PAY DIRT

BENNETT DYNASTY

BOOK 2

Kate Allenton

Published by Coastal Escape Publishing

Discover other titles by Kate Allenton
At http://www.kateallenton.com

Chapter 1

Twenty subpoenas served.
Ten bail jumpers found.
Five death threats.
And a partridge in a pear tree.
My stats from last month sounded like a bad Christmas carol.
The restaurant was one that herded people in and out during lunch hour like cattle. I'd skipped the hustle, bypassing tables of the business-suit-wearing people whose idea of conversation was spreading water cooler gossip. I'd headed straight for the U-

shaped bar, not to get sloppy drunk but to wait for my client.

There were two guys at the bar. The one closest to me made for magnificent scenery. His mussed dark hair suggested he'd been running his fingers through the dark strands. The stubble on his face only emphasized his crystal blue eyes, deep dimples, and a menacing scowl. The poor guy looked like he was having a bad day, even though just looking at him had made mine better.

The other patron sitting across from me was much more interesting. Not in an attractive way but a way that would pay out benefits. Some women might consider his award-winning smile, styled hair, and spray tan appealing. I wasn't one of them. He'd been nursing a beer until a plate with a hamburger and fries was placed in front of him.

I didn't like sitting at the bar alone. It felt awkward, made me fidgety, and implied I had no friends. I let only a handful of people into my world if you didn't count my plethora of sisters. It was easier to keep my family secrets contained that way.

An unfounded unease fluttered in my stomach, a feeling I couldn't quite place. A loud staccato beat rose above the normal restaurant noise as I tapped my foot on the barstool and rechecked my watch. He was late.

My gaze crossed the busy room and landed on the door. People walked in as others walked out. None of them the man I was waiting on. Rubbing my temples, I let out a long sigh.

Sometimes clients talked themselves out of believing in my ability to find things. Sometimes they didn't want to know the answers. I couldn't make them believe no matter how hard I tried, but this client was a repeat customer.

My regular clients called or met at my house, but this one was different. Unusual. Difficult. Challenging. This case was one I liked because it lacked the boring elements such as missing keys or jewelry. It was the weird ones that would consume me, engulf me, almost to where I'd forget my sister's obsession with believing our baby sister, Talia, wasn't dead.

Picking this restaurant had been strategic, easy, convenient, and it provided me the ability to deal with two problems at once.

Twenty minutes turned in to forty-five. The afternoon lunch crowd started to wind down. The guy sitting across from me had just discarded his napkin next to his plate and pushed them toward the bartender.

I pulled ten dollars out of my oversized purse and slid it across the scarred bar with one more appreciative glance at the sexy man who'd been sitting next to me, wishing he might meet my gaze. Not even a nibble as he nursed his soda. I decided it was now or never to get my other job done.

I rose and rounded the barstool, pulling out an envelope and my cell phone as I went. I smiled at the fake-tan man on the other side of the bar as I approached. His hamburger was half eaten, his French fries gone, only a goop of ketchup left in their place. He'd put his used napkin on the bar and had a single sip of beer remaining in his tall glass.

"Aren't you Bill Tanner?" I asked, as if I were a weather groupie fan girl from watching him on the six o'clock news. I could have predicted the weather with a better success rate just by flipping a coin.

A smile slid onto the man's face. His glazed eyes told me enough. He'd had a few more alcoholic beverages before I even arrived. His hungry gaze, previously pointed at the food remaining on his plate, had settled on the swells of my D-sized breasts.

I could work with the unwanted looks, even if it meant I'd need a shower when I got home. I batted my long eyelashes and tried for a sexy smile. The mirror above the bar showed that I was failing. My sexy smile looked like my old high school picture when I had been forced to say cheese before the flash blinded me.

"Yep. Are you a fan?" he answered and rested his unwanted palm on my hip. He licked his lips, never meeting my gaze, only my chest. "You want my autograph, sweetheart, or something more… filling."

Not likely, douchebag. Although he wore several rings, his wedding ring was absent. A conspicuous tan line stood out like a beacon, and I was familiar with his story. I wasn't a first-timer.

"How about we take this somewhere more private?" he asked, but paused as if he thought better of the offer. "You aren't a reporter, are you?"

"I'm not a reporter *or* a hooker, Mr. Tanner."

"Great, so what's it going to take?"

"Mr. Tanner, I'd love to take a picture with you. Maybe then you can give me your number. My sisters will be so jealous I got to meet you."

"Sure, sugar." He chuckled.

I turned in his arms, holding out my phone camera as he groped my booty. I lifted the envelope to get it in the picture before I turned back. Pressing the envelope against his chest, I leaned in to whisper, "You've been served."

His mouth gaped open before he snapped his lips together in a thin line. His laser-focused anger was pointed directly at me, and his bronze face turned blotchy red.

"Tell that bitch I'll kill her before she ever receives a dime," he growled as he rose from his seat. Snatching my shoulder, he spun me around. My dress strap ripping was loud in my ear.

My heartbeat pounded, and my body tensed. "Expect my testimony about the death threats in your divorce hearing. Your wife will get full custody of little Matt and Joey."

"You bitch." His fingers dug deeper into my shoulder, and his strike came quick and fast as he backhanded me across the cheek, making my cheekbones feel like they'd exploded. His rings cut my lip, and everyone in the restaurant paused, unmoving, as if not believing what they were witnessing. No one came to my aid.

"I guess your temper is why she's divorcing you?" I said, spitting blood from my lip. "Touch me again, and your wife won't have to worry about divorcing you. She'll get everything when you're dead. You understand?" I leaned into him and lifted my knee hard and fast into his family jewels, inflicting some deserved pain.

He dropped to his knees, cupping his crotch as I grabbed a napkin from the bar and blotted the blood pooling on my face while glancing around the ceiling. I grinned as I turned back to Tanner as he was trying to stand. "You're over." Before I could gesture to the cameras, Tanner pulled a gun and had his finger on the trigger.

I lifted my hands in the air. "You don't want to shoot. You'll do hard time for murder."

A snarl registered on his face as his eyes narrowed. He'd cocked the trigger when a mountain of muscles flashed by, pushing me out of the way as he tackled Tanner to the ground.

We all landed in a hot mess on the ground. My dress officially was ruined from the sticky goo on the floor.

Muscles met my gaze. The soda drinker pulled Tanner's hands behind his back. "FBI, and you're under arrest."

"FBI?" I questioned as he put the metal bracelets on Tanner. Had they had this guy under surveillance for more dirt?

"FBI?" Tanner asked. "Why the hell are you guys involved in a civil dispute? I haven't done anything."

Several men rushed into the restaurant. Most wearing bulletproof vests with FBI inscribed across the chests. A tall guy with balding hair had his hand resting on his gun. "What the hell did you do?"

"I served attorney papers," I answered.

"Not you," he growled and jabbed his finger toward a barstool.

Another officer guided me to the stool to sit.

"He hit her, Campbell," the mountain of muscles answered, passing the weatherman off to another agent.

Tanner's arrest would make the evening news. Too bad he wouldn't be wouldn't be following up with the weather forecast.

"And she fought back," Campbell answered. "Murray, you should have just broken it up and escorted him out. But no... you just had to break your cover and be a savior."

"Uh... I didn't need a savior, but thanks for trying, Murray, is it?" I said from the barstool.

They both glared at me. I had that effect on some people.

"You most likely scared Miss. Bennett's accomplice away."

"Wait, what?" I asked as I hopped off the barstool. How had I turned into the criminal and part of an FBI sting?

Campbell pointed to the seat I'd vacated. "You sit. I'll deal with you in a minute."

I was in the twilight zone. I fired off a text to my sister Gwen. *The FBI is about to arrest me. Can you do your thing?*

I started to sing my revised Christmas jingle again.

Twenty-one subpoenas served.

Ten bail jumpers found.

Six death threats.

And one… ruined FBI sting…

I dunked my scratchy napkin in a tall glass of water and dabbed at my bloody lip. The abrasive scratches on my arm stung. My favorite dress was torn at the shoulder strap.

Campbell stepped around my sexy-soda-drinking-linebacker and grabbed my phone before dangling a pair of handcuffs in front of me.

I held out my wrists and smiled. "You should think twice about this."

"Yeah, and why is that?" Campbell asked.

"Because I'm the victim here, and you'll get some bad press."

"I'm not worried about bad press," he said while he tightened the cuffs on my wrist.

"You might not be worried about the press, but you should be concerned that I had time to text my sister." I grinned even brighter as he yanked me off the barstool and escorted me out with Agent Murray following behind.

Chapter 2

I sat idly in an interrogation room. The sheriff's department knew me well. Not that I got in trouble a lot, but sometimes trouble found me when I was working on my cases. They knew what I was capable of, especially the sheriff. Finding Mrs. Sheriff's diamond ring had kept me in the man's good graces.

FBI Special Agent Campbell passed me off to one of the local detectives that I'd known for years.

Detective Jimbo Jones was a big man and intimidating on the outside but nothing but a teddy bear, all squishy and filled with fluff on the inside. He had a heart of gold and a demeanor that could scare sharks. I felt safe and untouchable.

Jimbo had led me into an interrogation room and had now returned with a first aid kit and latex gloves on his hands.

"What did you do?" he whispered as he dabbed rubbing alcohol on my face, making me wince.

"I served the News Channel 6 weather guy with divorce papers and got attacked in the process."

"He's got a rap sheet of domestic abuse a mile long, but his wife always drops the charges." Jimbo sighed. "Why did the feds bring you in, if it was an assault case?"

"I was hoping you could tell me."

He glanced back at the two-way mirror before leaning in and putting a bandage on my cut cheek, making me hiss through clenched teeth.

His voice was low and gravelly. "They haven't told us anything yet, but the sheriff knows you're here."

"Thanks, Jimbo." I rested my hand on his. "I texted Gwen before they took my phone away."

His eyes widened. Hearing my sister's name had that effect. She was like a category 5 hurricane when provoked, pissed and destroying everything in her way. "Gwen is coming here?"

"Yeah, sorry about that, but the feds think I have an accomplice to a crime I didn't commit."

The door opened again. Sheriff Tom Harrington walked in, his assessing gaze held mine as he cataloged the bruises and marks on my body. When it landed on my ripped dress, his jaw clenched. "You okay, Cassie?"

I nodded. "I was just serving divorce papers, Sheriff."

"Did the news reporter rough you up?"

"She was handling herself just fine," Agent Campbell said as he entered behind Sheriff Harrington.

"So, you saw it?" Harrington asked.

"We were watching the whole thing on the closed-circuit surveillance cameras."

Harrington turned his full gaze on Campbell, pegging him with his scrutiny. Feds might outrank local jurisdiction, but Harrington had a way of putting men in their place. Especially ones he didn't like. We had that in common. "Someone assaulted an innocent woman and almost shot her and you didn't do a damn thing?"

"Actually," I interjected, "the other FBI guy hurtled over the bar and tackled Bill Tanner before he could kill me."

Frowning, Harrington turned back to me. "It's not like you to miss something as important as a weapon."

"I know, right?" I said with widened eyes.

"Sheriff, do you mind?" Campbell asked.

"Right," he said. "Cassie Bennett, these men are from the FBI. Special Agents Ron Campbell and Nathan Murray. They need to ask you some questions."

I rubbed at my wrist. "Does the FBI put all of their witnesses in handcuffs?"

"Only the ones involved in our case."

"Cassie Bennett is a skip tracer, among other things. We've contracted out to her to help in investigations, so whatever you believe she did, there's probably more to the story than you realize."

Nathan Murray was a man to be reckoned with. He towered over me. Both men watched me as they sat down. But Murray's gaze had a way of caressing me, making my heart race in a guilty way.

He nodded in that official way that told me changing my clothes was still a long time coming before he sat down.

The sheriff stepped back and was about to close the door when I called out, "Tom, I'm sorry."

"For what, Cassie?" he asked.

"I texted Gwen."

Sheriff Harrington let out a heavy sigh. "Thanks for the heads-up."

The door shut behind him. His voice was muffled as he barked orders.

"So, would anyone care to tell me why the Feds were watching me?" I asked.

"We'll be the ones asking the questions; you'll be the one giving answers," Campbell said.

I sat back and winked at whoever was watching behind the two-way glass. If I didn't know better, my sister was probably already back there, along with her boyfriend, the attorney.

"Aren't you going to read me my rights?" I asked.

"You aren't under arrest," Murray answered, earning a glare from his compadre.

"Okay, so what am I doing here, and why did you haul me into the station in handcuffs?"

"Who were you meeting at the restaurant?"

"A client," I answered.

"What services are you providing him?" Campbell asked.

"Nothing illegal," I answered honestly.

"Who were you meeting, and what was the job?"

I crossed my arms over my chest and shook my head. "I'm a tracker, a skip tracer, but I find more than just people. I locate things."

"Like drugs for criminals?"

I clicked my tongue. "I won't do anything illegal. My clients know that up front. I do my homework, gentlemen, and even if one were to dupe me into finding something for them that was illegal, I'd turn the contraband into the police. I've already proved that before."

Campbell flipped open a file and read from it.

"Says here you're like a mind reader or psychic. How exactly does that work when people want you to find things?"

"It will be easier just to show you than explain. Give me your ring." I held out my hand toward Campbell.

"I'd rather you explain," he answered as he twisted the ring in question on his finger.

"Listen, you wanted answers, and this is me giving you answers." I shrugged. "You'll never believe me unless I show you, and I can't do that if you aren't willing to play."

"You're a fraud," Campbell said.

"If you say so," I answered with a smile.

Nathan Murray slipped a ring off his finger and handed it across the table. "What are you going to do?"

"I'm going to find the person who gave you that ring," I answered. Within seconds, a vision popped into my mind. A cemetery with weathered headstones and several dimes buried in the ground. I frowned and glanced down at a woman's platinum ring. "I'm sorry for your loss."

"Explain," he answered.

I gestured to the ring. "The person who gave that to you, or owned it before you, is deceased in a cemetery and surrounded by dimes. To be any more detailed, I'd need my map to pinpoint the location."

"She's right." Nathan Murray's gaze softened.

Sheriff Harrington opened the door and let Gwen and FBI Agent Fillpot into the room.

"I was sure you'd bring Max instead of him," I said as I rose.

"Max is in court, or I would have." Gwen's gaze landed on my busted lip then lowered to my torn dress. "Who did that to you?"

"It's nothing," I said. "The other guy took it worse."

Fillpot flashed his credentials. "She's one of mine."

"No, I'm not," I protested.

"The entire Bennett family is being watched by my division. Whatever you think she did, she didn't."

Gwen took me by the arm and was about to lead me out when I paused and turned back toward Nathan. I handed him his ring. "Thanks for offering to save me. Not that I needed it, but I still appreciate it."

"Not that you needed it," Nathan said.

"Wait, we weren't done here," Campbell called out.

"Yes, you are," Fillpot said. "The director is expecting your call."

We'd made it out into the parking lot before Gwen started in. "Serving subpoenas again?"

"Don't start," I said, glancing around and realizing that my car was still at the restaurant. "I was killing two birds with one stone and handling both my client and the papers at the same time. Only my client was late."

"Why did the FBI pick you up?" Gwen asked as she yanked open the passenger door to her car.

"I don't know. You didn't leave me in there long enough to find out."

Fillpot strolled up before Gwen could shut the door. "One of your clients was murdered."

"Which one?" I asked.

"I don't know yet."

Chapter 3

After a restless sleep, I rose the next morning and showered, taking extra care of my wounds. Overnight, the dark purple bruise under my right eye had turned a yellowish green tint. My lip bore an angry jagged line where Tanner's ring had split it open. I looked rough. I lifted my mug and hissed at the sting. Aggravation seeped down my spine while I tried to drink my coffee using only the left side of my mouth.

I should've taken a picture. I should blow it up and add a section on my fridge of things not to do when working. Most times, I knew my mark as well as I knew my sisters. I studied their habits before approaching them. There was nothing ever left to chance. Except for yesterday.

Bill Tanner didn't even own a gun, much less have a license-to-carry permit.

I stood at the fridge staring at pictures of past clients. They all smiled, holding up objects that I'd helped find. The thought of one of them being dead rattled within my chest like pennies in a Mason jar. Was it my fault they'd gone looking in the first place?

A knock pulled me from my morbid thoughts. I turned and strolled to the door with coffee in hand and pulled it open. FBI Special Agent Nathan Murray stood on my porch.

"Here to put me in handcuffs again, Agent Murray?"

His gaze landed on my busted-up face. He flexed his hand and slid them into his pockets as if to stop reaching for my wounds. "I should have never let it get that far."

"I shouldn't have either, especially when there was a glass on the counter within reaching distance." No way would he have known I would get into a fistfight with a weather man who wore more rings than my grandmother. Unless of course, Agent Murray was prone to premonitions like my sister. "What are you doing here, Agent?"

"Nathan," he said, sliding his hands out of his pockets. "Can you spare a few minutes?"

"Sure." I stepped out onto my porch. The delicate floral smell of my rose bushes drifted to my nose on the morning breeze. One neighbor, dressed in a dark blue striped robe, ambled to his mailbox to get his newspaper with his faithful dog jogging happily by his side.

My neighborhood was quiet most days until Sundays when, like clockwork, members of each family would be out working in the gardens or lawn. I wasn't one of those people, but I'd wave on occasion.

"We didn't get to finish our questioning yesterday."

My ego fell like a sack of potatoes. Any hope he'd come to ask me out on a date fizzled and dried up like yesterday's sun showers over hot coals. The steam was apparently only one-sided. "How can I help?"

I sat on the swing, folding my legs beneath me, and sipped my coffee, waiting for him to find the right words.

"How long had Herbert Guillot been your client?"

"Is he the one who died?" I asked. Him being late made more sense.

"You know?"

"Fillpot told me it was one of them. He just didn't give me a name." I swallowed hard. "But to answer your question, I'd guess maybe two months, but I'd have to check to be sure of his first appointment."

"Do you remember what he was looking for the first time he came to you?"

"Sure, only because it was odd. It wasn't the typical lost piece of jewelry or missing relative. It was something more unique."

Nathan pulled a coin out of his pocket and held it between two fingers to show me.

It wasn't a coin from this century, heck, probably not even the last. It was pure gold and looked like a Spanish doubloon or one from a pirate treasure. I knew it. "Herbert wanted to see if I could locate more gold coins."

"And did you?" Nathan asked.

"You know the answer to that, Special Agent," I answered. "It was all over the newspapers. I'm just glad he kept my name out of the equation."

"It didn't upset you that he hadn't told the press that you were the person responsible for giving him the location?"

"Upset me?" I asked, taking a sip of my coffee. "He referred to me as his own personal compass. Like I told you yesterday, I don't mind helping people find things or missing people as long as it's legal. Herbert was more like an armchair treasure hunter. I just helped nudge him in the right direction. That's all."

Nathan sat down beside me on the swing instead of taking one of the other chairs. He slowly rocked us as I sipped.

"The reason we were at the restaurant was because we were following you."

"Why would you do that? My life is far from exciting." Most days I took client phone calls from my house. Only on occasion did I have appointments that had me leaving the confines of my walls. Not to mention once-a-week trips to the grocery store. How much fun or interesting could that be?

"Your name was in Herbert's appointment calendar. You were supposed to meet with him yesterday. We wanted to see if the killer would show in his place."

"I'm afraid I don't understand."

"Did you send Herbert on a quest to New Orleans?" Nathan asked.

"Well, yeah," I said as my stomach turned to rocks, much like those in my garden. "Herbert has been searching for loot from a bank heist ten years ago. He believed after talking to some psychic that the hundred-dollar bill with the bank dye that he'd recently come into possession of was part of the loot the robbers hid before they all died in a plane crash. He hired me to see if I could help him locate the rest. Do you know anything about the bank heist?"

"Yes," Nathan said tilting his head from side to side as if trying to ease the muscles in his neck.

"You know the story, then?" I asked.

"I know every last detail about that story. My mother was killed by the robbers."

"I'm sorry for your loss." I glanced down at the ring he was wearing on his pinky finger. "What does this have to do with me, and why would you believe a killer would show up at Herbert's appointment?"

"Herbert Guillot was found dead in New Orleans. He had the hundred-dollar bill with the dye on it in a hidden suit pocket."

"You don't think I sent him there to die, do you?"

The rocking stopped, and Nathan turned to stare at me. His look became serious. "Everything at the crime scene had been wiped. There was no DNA, except for one place. Someone closed his eyes and left a fingerprint behind."

"That sounds like someone he probably knew or someone who had remorse."

"We agree."

"I hope you catch the guy. Did you have the fingerprint in your system?" I asked as dread twisted in my stomach.

"Sort of. We don't have his name, but it was tied to another case," he said, clasping his hands together "The print belongs to a dead man, one of the bank robbers."

"You think one of the bank robbers that killed your mother is still alive?" I understood it now. Why Nathan was sitting on my swing and he hadn't brought his bald partner from yesterday. This was personal. The stakes on getting answers were just as high for Nathan as they probably were for Herbert's family.

"Yes, and we believe Herbert's killer is coming for you next."

"Why would you think that?" I asked as panic laced my veins. The morning breeze was not so lovely anymore as I tried to process this information.

"Mr. Guillot's appointment book had a page ripped out for the date of your meeting at the restaurant."

"If it was ripped out, then how did you know it was in there to begin with?"

"His calendar syncs with his computer and his internet cloud service."

"Am I in danger?" I asked.

"You're the only person who stands between a criminal and his freedom to hide in the wind with millions of dollars. I'd say you're in considerable danger. The question is, if you're willing to help me track the killer so I can catch him."

"Of course, I'm willing, ready and able," I answered.

"Even if it means leaving town with me?"
"Let me pack a quick bag."

Nathan
Chapter 4

He didn't know what he expected, but Cassie Bennett wasn't it. She wasn't about the money. She could have demanded half of Herbert's find or even lied and gone to find the money herself.

She wasn't like that. She wasn't like that at all.

Unusual, sure. Beautiful, absolutely. But a gold digger? He wasn't buying it. But that was what his partner, Campbell, believed.

Something had always struck Nathan as odd about the theft and what happened to the robbers. He wasn't inclined to believe that karma played out. Only three bodies were found in the plane's wreckage, leaving one suspect unaccounted for. His superiors believed animals ravaged the other body, considering the plane had crashed into the side of a mountain. He was never even convinced the fourth one was on the plane to begin with.

He'd met many women who claimed to be a psychic and she'd offered him a reading. He'd put a few of her kind in jail. Cassie's reading of the ring had proven she had some type of skills.

There was no insignia or inscription on the ring he wore on his pinky. Nobody knew whom it belonged to, including Campbell. But Nathan knew. He'd visited his mother's grave once a month. And each time he was there, he promised the same thing. Not to find peace, love, and happiness but to find closure and bring all involved to justice.

Cassie jogged downstairs, pulling a suitcase behind her. "My sisters are going to be upset that I left town before waiting on our important package."

"What package?" he asked.

"A family heirloom that my relatives need me to tap into to find the rest of us crazy Bennett nuts."

"Sounds important," he said, trying to inject sincerity into his tone.

She patted his shoulder. "It's okay, Nathan. I'll get one of my sisters to pick it up."

"Keeping our destination a secret will help keep our location off the grid. The less the killer knows the better."

Cassie crossed the room and pulled open a filing cabinet. "And you're sure we need to go to New Orleans?"

"I'm not sure of anything," he said as he slipped an evidence bag out of his pocket and dangled it from across the room. "Do you believe that's where the money is?"

She crossed the room and took the evidence bag from Nathan's hand and examined it front and back. The red dye splatter covered enough of the bill to make it unusable. "May I open it?"

"Sure. You've seen that one before. That's Herbert's bill. I was surprised that the killer didn't find it on him."

"Maybe to throw you off your game. Could be that he wanted you to think Herbert was one of the robbers."

"Maybe." He slid his hands into his pocket, hoping she could pinpoint the location just as she had the fact that his mother was in a grave.

The truth was they'd run out of leads years ago, until one of the bills with the stolen serial number resurfaced again. He needed this. He needed her for answers.

"How long is this going to take?" he asked, following her across the room to the dining table where a map was already opened and laid out.

"You're nervous." She said it as more of a statement than a question.

Damn right, he was nervous. He gave her a curt nod and folded his arms across his chest.

"Normally I like to do this more than once just to be sure," she answered, slipping a necklace from around her neck. She held it over the map, closed her eyes, and forced out a sharp exhalation.

Nathan watched, trying to understand her ritual. Trying to make sense of how this might be possible. He drew a blank the longer he waited.

The crystal arced in circles as she moved it back and forth over the map of all fifty states. He had no idea what was going on in her mind, what she might be thinking, but she rubbed her thumb on the tainted money, and the crystal landed with a clank on the table.

She and Nathan both leaned in to read their next destination.

"Well, it looks like your money grew legs and moved, because it's in Texas now."

"You're sure?" he asked.

"The crystal doesn't lie. Give me a minute, and I'll try to narrow it down."

He nodded. This was worse than he thought. Cassie crossed the room and pulled a book off her bookshelf. She walked back over to the table and opened an atlas, flipping until she got to a map of Texas.

"This should point us to our mystery town. I don't have any detailed Texas town maps that give us streets, but hopefully, wherever we land, we can find one when we get there."

She did the same thing over again. Her crystal dangled over the map, and Nathan couldn't watch. He turned his back to her and paced away while rubbing his jaw. When it landed with a thud, he turned around.

"Tell me it isn't Millville."

She leaned in to read it and met his gaze. "How did you know?"

"That's where I grew up and where the robbery occurred."

Her mouth parted, but she didn't have to say a word.

"If you're returning home and the robber is still there, you're going to spook him."

"No, I'm not. I return home once a month, and this month is special."

"Why is that?"

"The annual domestic abuse ball. My mom was a major supporter of the cause, and my sister is competing in a rodeo. Double the reasons for a visit."

"Okay, just one teeny tiny question," Cassie said, holding up her pointer finger.

"What's that?"

"How are you going to show up with me? A complete stranger."

"That's easy. You can be a girlfriend."

"Do you bring many of those home to meet the family?"

He rubbed the stubble on his chin. "No, but that's the reason everyone in town will buy it."

"And how do we explain this?" she asked, pointing to her busted lip and black eye.

"The truth. You were serving a subpoena and got hit by accident. We don't need to alter your life at all. Just include me in it."

"Are you sure the killer didn't show up yesterday?"

He shrugged. "We've reviewed the footage and didn't notice anyone familiar or suspicious."

"If you're sure he took the appointment information, then he has my name, and it wouldn't be hard to find out what I look like."

"You're right. A hot beautiful blonde wouldn't be hard to spot in a crowd."

"You think I'm beautiful." A smile claimed her lips and lit her eyes. "Don't answer that." Cassie rubbed her fingers together. "If we're going to pull this off, we needed an expert in all things chameleon. My sister Gwen will help."

KATE ALLENTON

Chapter 5

Gwen thought she was doing me a favor in trying to talk me out of going to Texas, but she wasn't successful. I was going whether she liked it or not. That was why Nathan was standing in her living room and I was with her in the bedroom. She kept peeking out the door.

"What the hell were you thinking in bringing him here?" Gwen whispered.

"You're the only that I trusted to transform me," I answered over the sound of the hairdryer. My once-blonde tresses were now brown, similar to Gwen's. "I forgot to ask, have you talked to Grams about Talia?"

Gwen worked as an agent for Fairy Damn Godmother. They were like bodyguards when they needed to be, and Gwen was their resident chameleon. If anyone could change my appearance into something other than my everyday-Jane self, it would be her.

"Grams isn't doing well. The doctors don't want us to upset her, so we aren't allowed to raise her blood pressure."

"Not well?" I asked, peeking my head out. "Should I stay?"

"Personally, I think this is just another one of her ruses because she doesn't want to have the difficult conversation about why she didn't tell us Talia may still be alive."

"Can't say I blame her, that is if she knew anything about it. I'll check in on her when I get back from helping the FBI."

"Cassie, I know you can protect yourself. After all, I taught you. But don't you think this is taking things a little too far? You aren't FBI. And you're walking straight to where this killer is. That's not smart."

"Cassie Bennett isn't smart," I answered as I stepped out of her bathroom. The red sundress hit mid-thigh. The wide-brimmed hat sat low on my head with my now brunette tresses curled beneath. The actress-sized sunglasses sat on my nose. "But my new identity is smart and daring. Wait, what's my new name?"

Gwen rested her hands on her hips and whistled. "Damn, you look hot."

I clapped my hands together in a giddy-schoolgirl kind of way when Gwen walked into the bathroom and came back out, holding bold red lipstick, a shade she knew I'd never wear. She shoved it into a purse I'd left on the bed.

"I want *you* to be smart." She opened the bedroom door and exchanged my suitcase for one she already had packed in her closet. "In order for you to pull off being someone else, you have to play the part."

"Special Agent Nathan Murray, I'd like you to meet Cassie Newman."

"Newman? Are you serious?" I asked.

Gwen chuckled.

"Cassie, you look different, and what's wrong with Newman?" he asked, missing the inside joke.

A knock sounded on the door as I answered. "Newman is the last name of my first boyfriend."

"She used to practice writing his name," Gwen called out as she answered the door, returning moments later opening a brown envelope. She grinned as she handed me the documents. "Cassie Newman, you're now unofficially official."

"Newman," I repeated, letting the name roll off my tongue, trying to get used to it. Cassie Newman. Not as exciting as James Bond, but it would do. I thumbed through the documents. There was a passport, a driver's license, and a platinum credit card. I held it up.

Nathan shifted uncomfortably. "You know using forged paperwork is against the law without government approval."

Gwen shrugged. "If it comes down to it and you need the approval. I can get it. But you're going to need all the necessities to pull it off. Be sure to use it once or twice before you get there. You need to get used to signing your name. Stick as close to the truth as possible so that you'll remember the details. You two met while working a case. Cassie was attacked, and Nathan saved her."

"Wait, he didn't save me."

"It's true. I didn't save her."

Gwen sighed. "I know, but it's more romantic that way, and it lends credibility to the idea of Cassie being an easy target."

"And I'll kick his ass." I grinned.

"No, you're not kicking ass. If there's any ass-kicking to do, that's my job," Nathan said.

Gwen high-fived me in passing. We both knew who would be doing the deed. "I'll have a car waiting to pick you up at the airport. The driver will give you everything else you need, Cassie, including a gun and some cash."

"I hope you have a permit to carry a gun," Nathan said.

"She will before the plane hits the runway," Gwen said with a smile.

"You've thought of everything." I squeezed my sister tight, knowing she hated it when I invaded her personal space.

"I'll pick up the package Abby is sending you, and when you get back, we can start trying to hone in on Talia and the other Bennett line.

"Who are Talia and Abby?" Nathan asked.

"She can explain on the plane ride." Gwen shoved us toward the door with the new luggage. "Oh, one more thing." Gwen ran to her room and returned with a pair of diamond stud earrings and a diamond bracelet.

"I don't know about this, Gwen. I might lose these." I gawked as Gwen fastened the bracelet to my wrist.

"I'd give you the diamond necklace, but we both know you won't remove your crystal."

She was right. I never took that thing off and for a good reason. "What if I lose them?"

"It's okay, Cassie. They're insured. Besides, you find things."

The flight was in coach. Nathan offered me the window seat. It was only then that he told me that he'd taken this time off to follow up on the lead. That there wouldn't be any FBI backup or people in play. We were totally going into this alone.

When the plane touched down, we were met by a man holding a sign that read *Newman*. I would have walked right passed him had Nathan not nudged me and leaned in to whisper in my ear. "Isn't that you?"

"Cassie Newman?" the driver asked as we approached.

The other people waiting for their loved ones were more down-home casually dressed in wide-brimmed cowboy hats. We'd been greeted with a chauffeur wearing an expensive suit. Apparently, we weren't going to blend in.

"Yes."

"Clayton Michaels, FDG." He grinned and took my carry-on bag, sliding the strap up his shoulder. "I'll be your driver while you're in town, and I've booked our rooms at a local hotel. Neither Gwen or Mrs. Delany informed me if you had reservations."

Clayton was a pretty boy. His dark chocolate hair perfectly coifed. His designer suit without a single wrinkle. His smile was filled with mischief, but if what I knew about FDG was true, this man had some secret kick-ass technique that he hid beneath his well-mannered vibe.

"Oh, we don't need reservations. We're staying at the farm." Nathan said.

"A farm?" Clayton asked.

"Yeah, my daddy's farm, but don't worry. He's got an extra room for you too."

Chapter 6

"I couldn't possibly impose," Clayton said.

Nathan patted Clayton on the back. "I'll feel better with another agent around to watch her back."

"Great," Clayton said, as if he'd just been told he needed a root canal. "Please tell me your father doesn't have farm animals. I'm allergic to them."

"Which ones?" I asked as the conveyor started to move and the luggage began to come through.

"All of them," Clayton answered.

I wasn't sure if my sister even realized how much she'd missed the mark on sending Clayton to be our driver. He was dressed as if he were off the New York runway and not someone that might step in horse manure.

We strolled out through the electronic doors. The smoldering heat smacked my face like a sopping dishrag, and pressed heavily on my chest. The sun seemed about five times brighter than in my hometown. A limo was parked outside. It contrasted with all the other vehicles, mainly consisting of beat-up pickup trucks and four-wheel drives. People in the distance rode on horseback, corralling sheep.

"Aren't we going to stand out in that thing?" I asked.

'Your sister insisted on the best." Clayton said.

Nathan grabbed for the door handle, but Clayton knocked his hand away. "I'm the chauffeur. At least let me do my job."

"I'm sorry that my sister got you into this," I said, sliding inside onto the leather seats.

Clayton poked his head in to meet my gaze. "I owed her. She saved my life. The least I can do is watch out for her sister."

Nathan slid in next to me while Clayton loaded the luggage in the trunk. "You sure do have an interesting family."

"My life was boring, but that all changed when Fillpot showed up in town. See, my sisters and I all have unique abilities, and now Special Agent Fillpot has convinced Gwen that our baby sister is still alive. He has her hunting a ghost she can't ever expect to find."

"Crazy genes and all, I appreciate you helping. We ran out of leads a long time ago until one of the bills resurfaced."

I understood the need for closure. When my parents and sister died, I'd been lost in a dazed whirlwind trying to process the overwhelming grief. I knew what it meant to need things finalized in order to breathe.

I glanced out the window, taking in the scenery. Millville, Texas, was exactly like I thought it would be after looking at it from in the sky. The vast openness of the land catered to farm equipment and tumbleweeds. The town was clumped together in one area with tendrils that reached farther out for those who didn't enjoy congregating with people.

I refocused on Nathan. "If you grew up here, you must know everybody in town. Do any of them strike you as bank robbers?"

He shook his head and turned his gaze out the window. "Not a one, but if I find out one of them was responsible for my mother's death, it's going to be hard not to take justice into my own hands."

The window between the driver's compartment and the back lowered as the car was started. Clayton glanced in the rearview mirror. "Gwen told me you two just met. You're sitting too far apart to be a happy romantic couple. You might want to get the awkwardness out of the way while behind the tinted windows." Clayton chuckled as the window rose again, blocking us off from his commentary.

"He's right," I said. I slid the dress up my legs and climbed onto Nathan's lap.

His body tensed with my unexpected action, but relaxed as he grinned. His palms rested on my hips. "You don't have a shy bone in your body, do you?"

"In my line of work, I've had to play all kinds of parts to get close to my targets to serve papers or sweet talk information on my bail jumpers. Granted, it didn't involve climbing onto laps, but I'm a closet actress. I don't just help Nancys looking for their lost car keys." I smiled, staring into his eyes. "Kiss me."

Nathan swallowed uncomfortably as he met my gaze, but that didn't stop him from following through on my demand. His hand rested on my lower back. His lips met mine, slow and sensual. He kissed me like a man savoring my taste until he broke the kiss and leaned his forehead against mine. Our heated breaths mingled.

"There's something I need to tell you."

"Hold that thought," I said seconds before I kissed him like I meant it. There was nothing slow or essential about the way I took his lips, devouring him and tasting him in a single breath. I pressed my body against him as desire pulled within me. His hand on my back slid into my hair, tilting my head, giving him better access. Our erratically beating hearts matched until I broke the kiss.

His gaze lingered on my lips as we both fought to catch our breaths. "That was hot."

He opened his mouth and then closed it again. His hands still holding onto me, he leaned in and kissed me again as if he'd needed just one more kiss to validate the heat sizzling between us.

The feeling was mutual.

He pulled away, and I climbed off his lap, fanning myself. "It's hot in Texas."

"I think you just made it ten times warmer," Nathan said, clearing his throat.

"Okay, we can pull off chemistry. So what did you want to tell me?"

"My family is as unusual as yours."

"Ooooh," I cooed. "Do they have abilities too?"

He chuckled. "Not quite, but you'll see."

The conversation ended as the limo pulled beneath a metal arch that read Murray Ranch. The road was bumpy, but I stared out the window. Where I'd expected farm animals and barns, there was a gated area with men working around large metallic equipment plunging down into the earth, thrusting like a man thrusting his hips in the heat of passion.

"What in the world?"

"That's an oil rig," Nathan said as the car pulled up to the three-story house with three beat-up pickup trucks parked outside. "I said my momma was killed at the bank, not that she worked there."

KATE ALLENTON

Chapter 7

Clayton opened the door, and Nathan slid out, extending his hand toward me. "Well played, Agent Murray. When you said farm, I didn't see this coming. Maybe it *would* be better if I stayed out here."

Nathan chuckled as he and Clayton rounded the vehicle to get the bags out. I cupped my hand over my eyes, shielding them from the sun as I gazed around the area. Trees lined one side of the house, which would create shade at sunrise. Toward the south, a oil rig was churning. In the other direction, the fields were empty for miles, with one exception—a barn in the distance with a gated area and a horse galloping inside the fence.

"You have horses?" I asked.

"Yeah, my sister rides them. She competes," Nathan said.

The screen door shoved open and banged off the house siding. A young woman wearing a cowboy hat came running out. She charged Nathan, and he'd barely dropped the suitcases in time before catching the young woman in his arms and lifting her in a hug off the ground.

"You didn't tell me you were coming."

"It was a last-minute decision," Nathan said and glanced up onto the porch. He gave a quick wave to the older man sitting on the porch in the shade watching us.

Nathan led the young woman over to me. "Squirt, this is Cassie. Cassie, this is my baby sister, Amanda."

Amanda held out her hand, and I shook. "Who beat you up?"

I'd almost forgotten about my bruises. Heat crept to my cheeks. "A man in a bar. He stole my French fries, but don't worry, he looks worse."

Amanda's brows dipped as she turned her glare on her big brother. "Was she with you? Did you let her get hit?"

"It was over before I could intervene. That's one of the things I love about Cassie. She doesn't need a man to save her." Nathan rested his arm over my shoulders.

Amanda's eyes widened. "You never bring girls home."

"She's special," Nathan answered.

"And who are you?" Amanda asked, glancing at Clayton.

"I'm the driver and her friend," Clayton answered.

"Am I being punked?" Amanda asked, walking to the back seat of the car. She yanked the door open and stuck her head inside as if expecting to find someone filming the entire exchange.

"No, squirt, you aren't being punked, so be nice," Nathan said, grabbing the suitcases. "Come on, you guys, let me show you where we're sleeping."

Amanda wrapped her arm around mine and led me to the porch. "He didn't tell you about us, did he?"

Heat climbed to my cheeks. "He's been busy with work, and so have I."

I tried to stick as close to the truth as possible as Gwen had schooled me, but something told me that little Ms. Amanda had a keen eye, just like her FBI agent brother.

"Amanda, give her some room to breathe. You've got plenty of time to drill her."

"It's not me you should worry about." Amanda chuckled as she disappeared inside the house.

Introductions to the old man on the porch went smoother. Nathan's granddaddy had hardly said a word while chewing on his unlit pipe.

Nathan showed us inside the house. I'd been expecting doilies and well-worn furniture, and I would've been half right. As spacious as this house was, it had every bit of southern charm imaginable, all the way to the smell of homemade apple pie.

"This place is fabulous. I'm surprised you ever left here."

Nathan guided us up to the second floor. "Cassie will be sleeping in my room down the end of the hall. Clayton, feel free to take any room on this floor. This floor is for guests. The rest of the family sleeps on the third floor."

"You sleep on the guest floor?" I asked as I followed behind Nathan with Clayton disappearing into one of the rooms as we passed.

"I'm never home, so it makes sense," Nathan said, opening the wide double doors at the end of the hall. I paused under the doorframe. It wasn't just a room we were standing in. It was a suite, complete with a sitting area. "This is bigger than my first apartment."

"I'm glad you approve." Nathan chuckled and dumped the suitcases on the bed. "I'll take one of the couches, and you can have the bed."

"No need. I'm not a prude. I have no modesty. I grew up with seven sisters, counting Talia."

I slipped my hat off my head and turned to find a woman standing in the doorway.

"I had to see it with my own eyes."

Nathan glanced over his shoulder at the woman and grinned. "Mildred, you're looking as beautiful as ever." He crossed the room and lifted the woman in a bear hug.

There was nothing petite and helpless about Mildred. She was one of those women who oozed organization with a motherly persona. Her gaze was assessing and unwavering, even as Nathan squeezed her tight.

"Had I known you were coming I would have made all your favorites."

"There's still time." Nathan chuckled. "Mildred, I'd like to introduce Cassie, my girlfriend."

"Aw." Mildred's face softened. "What happened to you, honey?" Mildred asked, touching air near my black eye as if she was afraid to make me hurt worse.

"It's silly, really. I'm a klutz, and when a man tried to steal my fries, I ran into his fist." I patted the woman's arms. "But it's fair. I think I broke his family jewels."

"A girl after my own heart." Mildred's smile grew as she pulled me into a hug. "Welcome, child. We're glad to have you."

"Thanks for having me," I said awkwardly.

"Your family must not be big huggers," Mildred said.

Seems she'd read my tense stance accurately. "I come from a big family, but there wasn't much physical contact. We weren't really brought up that way."

"Oh well, the longer you're here, the more we'll change that."

Mildred spun around and headed back out the door. "Dinner is in an hour. Bring your appetites."

Nathan spent the next hour bringing Clayton and me up to speed on the case. He'd had a copy of the complete FBI file that included everything about the robbery, the plane crash, and poor Herbert Guillot's death.

I would have had a hard time believing that Herbert's death was in any way tied to the missing bank money had a fingerprint not been found on his eyelids. None of us could explain how or why the cash had moved. It honestly didn't make sense.

"I can hack into the flight manifests to see if there were any locals arriving from New Orleans," Clayton said.

"That's a good idea. Can you also look into car rentals? I suspect he's local, but I could be wrong. It wouldn't hurt to check every angle."

"If he's local that's going to make it more difficult." Clayton said.

"I know. New Orleans is within driving distance. Since Amanda first started competing, my parents would load up the horse trailer and drive her over there. It's just a hop, skip, and a jump away."

My smile grew. "You've been in town for five minutes, and you've already reverted back to your country roots."

He chuckled. "Darlin, they never left. I've just learned to adapt."

Mildred tapped on the door. "Dinnertime."

"Thanks, Mildred, we'll be right down," Nathan called out.

Clayton clapped his hands together and grinned. "Time to put on your game faces and show them you're a couple."

Chapter 8

Nathan, Clayton, and I proceeded down the stairs toward the sound of voices and clinking silverware. My palms turned sweaty as a fluttery feeling overtook my stomach. I'd never had to play the role of girlfriend before. Sure, I'd dated, but playing the part with a man I barely knew anything about, other than he was a solid-ten kisser, was a first.

Nathan slipped his fingers through mine and squeezed as if sensing my turmoil just before we stopped in the dining room. A big rustic table with seating for twelve took up most of the room. A deer-antler chandelier hung from the ceiling, complete with added tear drop crystals from the antlers as if trying to make it look chic. It was nothing quite like I'd seen before and probably never would again.

Several men were already seated while Amanda and Mildred carried casseroles and serving dishes out of the kitchen.

"Well, don't just stand there, sit down, and get some food before it's all gone," the man, wearing a cowboy hat and sitting at the head of the table, said.

"No hats at the table," Mildred said, knocking the man's arm.

"Dad, I'd like for you to meet Cassie and Clayton."

"Um-hum," he said, loading his plate up with fried chicken. "Amanda and Mildred already filled me in."

"Guys, this is my dad, William Murray." Nathan pointed to the others at the table. "You already met Grandpa, but that's Pete and Joe. They help my dad with work on the rig."

I held up my hand. "Hi, and thanks for having me."

Nathan guided me to the table and pulled out a chair. Everyone's gaze followed, as if this had been a trick performed by a monkey instead of Nathan. Maybe it had been true that he never brought home girls.

"Well, dig in," Mr. Murray said, gesturing with a biscuit toward the other platters.

There was a sensory overload with the food. Country cooking at its finest. Everything from dumplings to fried chicken and all the southern veggies to go with it.

Clayton and I both filled our plates. The others watched in curiosity, especially William, Nathan's dad. It was as though he was waiting to see what I'd eat, as if each dish had its own meaning.

I didn't hold back. I took fried chicken, a heaping mound of mashed potatoes and gravy, a biscuit, and just a pinch of greens, trying to save room for that apple pie I'd smelled on the way in.

I could just imagine what he was thinking. Meat eater, check. Mashed potatoes and gravy, doesn't care about calories or carbs, check, check."

I must have passed his initial inspection because he turned his attention back to his own plate.

Talking around the table resumed after I took my first bite. The conversation revolved around the day in the field and how they believed the oil they'd tapped was starting to dry up and they'd have to move the rig to another place soon.

The chair at the end of the table sat empty. A single glass filled with wine sat in front of the chair. I'd expected Mildred to occupy the seat, but she never did.

William turned his gaze on Nathan. "We usually don't see you until the end of the month. Why did you deviate from your normal routine?"

Nathan had a mouth full of food and held up his finger to his dad because he couldn't answer. As I looked around this table, I thought there was no way they wouldn't see through my ruse.

As if Nathan knew I was about to spew the ugly truth, he stopped me by resting his hand around the back of my chair and took a big swig of his beer.

"I wanted to show Cassie where I grew up, and she's never been to a rodeo."

"And you?" William turned his gaze to Clayton. "Are you always their third wheel, or are they into some kinky shit where they like three-ways?"

Clayton coughed on his drink.

"William Murray, you know that Jenna, God rest her soul, would have your hide for talking to your son's guests that way." Mildred said as she took a seat.

"I'm just Cassie's driver."

"And best friend," I offered. "Clayton's never been to Texas, but he's fantasized about being a cowboy and learning the Texas two-step. Isn't that right?"

Before Clayton could even answer, Amanda started with her questions. "Why the limo? You trying to impress us or don't you know how to drive yourself?"

"Sure, she does. I'm just better at it," Clayton said.

William rose from the table. His plate was only half empty. "I bet Nathan never told you about my special ability."

I raised a brow. "No, sir."

He nodded and met his son's gaze. "I can spot a lie a mile away, so when you three are ready to tell me the truth about why you're here, you can find me on the porch."

Mr. Murray walked out of the dining room, and silence filled the air.

"Dad, wait," Nathan said as he pushed out of his chair.

I rose and stopped Nathan from following him. "Let me."

Nathan's gaze went over my head in the direction his father had gone before he met my gaze again. Hurt and anger filled his face.

"I've got this," I said and patted his arm before glancing at the table. "Save my plate, though." I grabbed a biscuit and walked out.

Mr. Murray was standing on the porch, staring out at the rig when I stepped up beside him. "One of my clients was killed, and that's what brought Nathan into my life."

"I hope you aren't still trying to tell me that you two are a couple."

"I'm not," I said and gestured to the rig. "Walk with me, and I'll explain."

William stepped off the porch, and we started in a slow stroll toward the equipment in the distance. "It would be easier if I start at the beginning for you to understand how we ended up at your door."

I proceeded to tell William everything, including the uncanny way I find people and other things. How all of my sisters are unique. I wasn't sure he was buying a word I said, because he'd remained quiet until we reached the rig.

"Did Nathan tell you why we bought this farm?"

"No, sir. He didn't even tell me we were coming to a farm until we arrived."

"I bought this land thirty years ago, after I married Nathan's mother, Jenna." She fell in love with the rose garden. She was the love of my life and still is." His voice softened, proving he was a man still in love with his wife. "That's why we place the wine glass at the end of the table during each meal. It's so if she's ever looking down on us, she knows we haven't forgotten her."

"I'm sure she was a special woman. I would have liked to have met her."

"She was an angel. She volunteered at a woman's shelter. She was an advocate against domestic abuse. She didn't have to work, but just like I put in my blood, sweat, and tears here on the ranch, she did that for other women." His gaze was trained in the distance, as if he the memories played like a movie in his mind.

"You mentioned the oil is going to dry up soon," I said, unlatching the gate. I stepped closer to the equipment, and William followed.

"Studies have indicated that it's inevitable."

I squatted and ran my finger through a puddle of black gold on the ground. Rubbing my fingers together in one hand, I clutched my crystal with the other. Glancing across the field, I grinned before I rose.

"So, what are you looking for, Ms. Newman?"

"My last name isn't Newman. It's Bennett, but let's keep that secret between us." I took his arm and started walking off in another direction, still holding the crystal in my hand.

With each step we took, the crystal's vibration increased as we approached. "Nathan has good reason to believe that one of Jenna's killers is still alive, and I've tracked the money back to this town."

William grabbed my arm. "That's why he brought you here?"

"Yeah, and he has money from the heist to prove it," I said and continued walking until the vibration in my crystal had traveled down my spine and through my body. I stopped and glanced around. Spotting a stick, I picked it up and moved back to where I'd been standing. I dug at the ground and shoved the stick into the hole. "You should consider moving the equipment over here." I held up my finger, showing him the oil from the other side of the field. "Yeah…I'd dig right here."

His brows dipped, and he crossed his arms over his chest. "You believe there's oil right there?"

I grinned. "I don't believe; I know it is." I grabbed another stick and placed it next to the first one, marking the spot with an X, as if it were a pirate's bounty. "Now X marks the spot. Dig there."

William rubbed his neck. "How is it you think you can find the money?"

"The same way I just made you a fortune."

"If there's oil there, I'll cut you in on it."

I led him back toward the house. "I don't want your money, Mr. Murray. I just may need your help in keeping the reason why we're here a secret. You see the killer might have seen me while I waiting on my client. Since then, I've dyed my hair, my sister made me fake documents, and we've gone through a whole lot of trouble to help your son. So, if you don't mind, please keep our secret, until we leave. I'd really like to help Nathan find the peace that's been eluding him."

"Did he tell you that?" he asked.

"I read it in his blue eyes."

"I'll keep your secret if you do one thing for me."

"The oil wasn't enough?" I asked with a chuckle.

"If you find the killer and he's a local, I want to know about it."

"I don't think—"

"Take it or leave it, Ms. Newman, or should I say, *Bennett*?"

I shook my head. "I'm afraid I can't do that. You're old school. You probably believe in an eye for an eye."

74

He pulled a handkerchief out of his pocket and wiped the oil from my fingers. "I won't kill him," he said, lifting his gaze to mine. "You have my word, just like you have my word we're splitting the profits on the oil."

Chapter 9

We headed back to the house. Everyone who'd finished eating was sitting on the porch, eyeing our approach as if William and I were their evening entertainment.

William gestured to the door. "Mildred, heat up our plates so Cassie and I can finish eating."

"All good?" Nathan asked as he stood.

William met Nathan's gaze. "Good enough for now. Next time, just warn me."

Nathan let out a long audible breath, and relief flooded his face. "Yes, sir."

William rested his palm on Nathan back. There was a knowing glint in his father's eyes.

This was a family who told each other everything. No secrets in this bunch. I envied the connection and felt horrible about the fact he'd been willing to lie.

"If your girlfriend is right, she's about to be rich. You might want to hang on to her before anyone else snatches her up."

Nathan's brows dipped. "But she told you…"

"I know what she told me, son. Cassie is an honest woman who's just here to meet your family. We're glad to have her."

Nathan gave me a questionable look as I followed behind William and Mildred back into the house.

"Come on, child. Let's heat up your food."

Nathan walked with me, leaning in to whisper, "Didn't you tell him?"

I nodded. "I told him everything. He's willing to go along with it."

Nathan snapped his mouth closed and pulled out my chair again. His father watched as we each sat at the table.

"No one needs to know the truth; besides, you picked a perfect week to have outsiders here."

"The rodeo," Nathan said, grabbing a biscuit and peeling it open.

"And your mother's benefit Saturday night. I hope you brought your tuxedo."

"Benefit?" I asked, trying to remember what Nathan had told me.

Mildred walked in, carrying a pitcher of tea. She refilled our glasses. "The Founder's benefit and auction. All proceeds go to a shelter to help women dealing with domestic abuse."

"This will be perfect," Cassie said.

"This isn't perfect, Cassie. There will be a lot more people in town, a lot more suspects, a lot more strangers I've never seen. This is the opposite of perfect," Nathan said.

I understood why he would think that, even though my brain wasn't wired the same way. In my job it was easier to go unnoticed, to get close to the target, and that was what we needed. In his job, criminals that stood out made it easier for him to make an arrest. The money was here. It was a simple question of where.

I smiled at Nathan and, beneath the table, rested my hand on his knee. "This is a good thing, Nathan. I'll get to meet everybody, and if our fun adventures take us off the beaten path, it will make sense. What do I know? I'm not from these parts."

Mildred crossed her arms over her chest and regarded us suspiciously. She raised a single brow. "Adventures and Nathan? Those two words are never used in the same sentence. Nathan is by the book. Every time a vacation was planned, Nathan was the one who had the entire travel itinerary typed up and ready to distribute. He doesn't know the word spontaneous." She glanced between both of us. "Nathan, I've known you since you were in diapers. Your mother and I taught you how to walk, talk, and two-step. You're not adventurous, and you never bring home women, much less women who have drivers. You don't encourage socialites, and you don't flaunt your money, so start explaining."

I rose from my seat and grabbed a napkin, loading it with a drumstick and another biscuit. I gestured over my shoulder. "I'm going to eat this on the porch. I'll let you guys…explain." I raised my napkin toward Mildred. "Love your cooking by the way. It's better than anything back home."

Obviously acting as a girlfriend was harder than acting as anything else when I'd tried to get close to people to serve papers. I probably should have taken lessons from Gwen growing up. I hadn't been in town more than a couple hours and people were already onto our lie. The only opinion that mattered to me was William's, Nathan's father. Once we cleared the air, I felt better about finding the money. I could track money, I could find things, but I couldn't fix broken families.

Pete and Ed were out in the field where I'd placed my pirate X-marks-the-spot sticks. Clayton was sitting in a rocking chair when I sat down on the swing. Amanda was missing in the wind. "I came clean to Nathan's dad. I think Mildred is trying to figure things out."

Clayton shook his head and continued in the slow sway of his chair. "You didn't even last a full day."

"I know," I added with a sigh. "I'm normally so much better than this when I have to get close enough to serve papers."

"Well, if it makes you feel any better, the oil workers think he just brought you home to hide you away. They think Nathan's saving you from an abusive relationship, thanks to your black eye and busted lip."

"So, in other words, I didn't fool anybody." My gaze went out to the barn. "Well, Amanda may have believed me."

"She doesn't. She's a teenager and already snapped your picture with her cell phone while you are eating dinner. If I had to guess, she'll upload it onto the Internet tonight and see if she gets any hits on familiar pictures."

My mouth parted, and words escaped me. How had I not even noticed that?

"Don't feel bad. These teenagers are going to rule the world one day, and I came prepared." Clayton pulled a magnet out of his pocket and held it up. "If it comes down to it, this sucker should erase her entire phone, including your picture."

"Genius," I whispered.

"I know." Clayton chuckled. "What's your take on Ed and Pete?"

"I wasn't around them long enough to get a feel about them one way or the other."

"What's so interesting about that ground where they're pointing?" Clayton asked.

"That's the next place that the Murray family is going to strike black gold."

"Oh…that's right. Gwen says her sisters each have abilities. I should have known that you'd have *something*."

"I find things. That's all."

"Expensive things?" Clayton wiggled his brows.

"Lost and missing things."

We were still out on the porch talking when Mildred appeared and handed me a glass of tea. She took a seat beside me and pushed the swing to get it moving again as Nathan came out onto the porch and sat in one of the rocking chairs.

We sat out on the porch until the moon rose in the sky and a million stars twinkled above. I'd never seen such beauty, not where I live, not anywhere. I was starting to understand why Texans loved the outdoors. I might, too, if I were able to play under this stage of lights.

"It's getting late, and we need an early start tomorrow." Nathan held out his hand, and I took it, letting him pull me up from the swing.

"Cassie, you can have your own room," Mildred called out.

I grinned like a woman on a mission. "It's fine. You guys might know the truth, but not everyone else does." I gestured to Ed and Pete.

"Right." Clayton wiggled his brows. "Keeping up appearances is part of the fun."

Nathan cleared his throat. "Right, well, good night."

Nathan guided me upstairs to his room. I grabbed some clothes and changed into a pair of boy shorts and a tank top. I came out of the bathroom, and Nathan was already in bed. He was wearing lounge pants and was shirtless. "I hope this is okay."

"Sure," I said, trying hard not to stare at his abs. I flexed my fingers when all I wanted to do was trace the indentions and kiss a path over his body. "No problem."

I crawled into bed and pulled the covers up. Nathan reached over me and turned off the light. His face was only inches from mine as he stared down at me. "Thanks for coming clean to my dad. I don't like lying to him."

"I didn't like lying to him either."

He leaned in and pressed a tender kiss to my lips, as if it were a nightly ritual. When he pulled back, he said, "I'm sorry."

I grinned. "I'm not. Just consider it practice for all of the locals we have to convince."

"Practice," he said as his gaze landed on my mouth.

I licked my lips.

He didn't move and stared down at me. His gaze slowly traveled north to my eyes. "Good night, Cassie."

Nathan rolled back over onto his side of the bed, proving he had more control than me. If I'd taken the lead, we wouldn't need separate sides of the bed; then again, we wouldn't be getting any sleep.

"I appreciate you helping me."

"If I hadn't helped Herbert Guillot, he might still be alive," I said as Nathan turned off the lamp on his side of the bed, plunging the room into darkness.

Another person dying because of my ability had shaken me. Serving subpoenas and notices to appear was one thing. It was only my wellbeing I had to be concerned with. I stared up at the unfamiliar ceiling and, for the first time ever, debated if I'd done the right thing.

Nathan
Chapter 10

Nathan rolled over in the bed to find Cassie had already gotten up. The door to the bathroom stood open, the light off. He rolled out of bed, grabbed a change of clothes, and headed straight for the shower. Cassie's shampoo and conditioner were sitting on the tub. The scent of strawberries hung in the air. A used towel draped the curtain rod.

He grinned. She'd made herself at home. How had he slept through it?

He showered and dressed and headed downstairs to find Mildred in the kitchen, doing dishes and staring out the window.

"Have you seen Cassie?" Nathan asked.

"You could say that," she said and gestured to the window.

Cassie was in the field with Nathan's dad. She was wearing a cowboy hat and was walking around with a can of spray paint, marking different areas in the yard. "What in the world is she doing?"

"Not sure, but I'm surprised William is letting her do it with spray paint."

A truck pulled up, and a man got out. A smile pulled at Nathan's lips. "Is that…"

"Your Uncle Dan," Mildred answered.

Dan and his son, Marty, got out of the truck. Marty headed straight for the barn and horse arena where Amanda was practicing. The two of them had been inseparable growing up. Marty was a good kid. A straight-A kid fresh out of high school. Uncle Dan wasn't really Nathan's uncle, but he might as well have been. He and Nathan's dad were best friends.

Uncle Dan ran the town bank. The same bank Nathan's dad used for his oil business. The same bank Nathan's mother visited on the day she died.

"Do Marty and Amanda still practice together?"

"If that's what the kids are calling it these days," Mildred answered and gestured toward the kitchen table. "I saved you and Clayton some breakfast. The rest of us already ate. Just heat it up."

"Did someone say breakfast?" Clayton asked, walking into the kitchen. He stepped up to the window and peered outside. "What is she doing?"

"There's no telling," Nathan answered.

He and Clayton made plates and took them into the dining room.

"Did you stay up late?" Nathan asked.

"I've been researching those flights and rentals."

"Find anything yet?" Nathan asked.

"Nothing of interest, but I'm only half way though." Clayton answered.

They were just finishing up when Nathan's dad, Uncle Dan, and Cassie walked in. She was pulling the hat off her head and using it to fan her red face.

Nathan recognized the hat, and he should. He'd bought it for his mom years ago. It had been her favorite. A hint of pride made him smile. It looked good on her. She looked like she fit right in.

"Well, there you are," Uncle Dan said, holding out his hand.

Nathan rose and shook it. "Uncle Dan, it's been a long time."

"Too long, son, but I'm glad you're back and that you brought your girlfriend and her friend. The more, the merrier."

"They came to see Amanda ride, and they're staying for the Benefit," Nathan's dad said.

"I wouldn't miss either of those for the world. I know how important they are to Nathan, right, baby?" Cassie said as she closed the distance and pressed a tender kiss on Nathan's lips while proceeding to steal his bacon.

Nathan snagged her around the waist and pulled her into his lap. He kissed her again and smiled into her face. "You look good in my mother's hat."

Cassie blushed a pretty pink. She was laying it on thick, and he could play his part. Hell, he wanted to play this part.

"Okay, you guys, keep it PG. There are teenagers outside," his dad said, stealing another piece of bacon as Cassie had just done. His father patted Nathan's shoulder. "I'm not kissing you for it."

Clayton covered and protected his plate from the others and moved to the other side of the table out of reach.

"I reserved our booth at the rodeo. You three should join us," Uncle Dan said.

"A booth?"

"It's the VIP area of the arena," Nathan explained.

"VIP. Now that I can get behind," Clayton said, pointing with his bacon before biting off a piece.

Clayton oozed manners and charm. Him being an FDG operative made sense. Nathan just hoped the man was as good with people as he was at watching Cassie's back.

Uncle Dan handed Nathan's dad an envelope. "All we need to close the deal is your signature to start the process. You can either drop it off at the bank or bring it to the rodeo if you don't have time."

"You didn't have to drive all the way out here to drop it off. I'd planned to come into town, but now that Nathan showed up, I've got to be here when the new rig shows up so I can pinpoint where to put it."

"New rig?" Nathan asked.

William grinned. "New rig." He chuckled and handed the bacon he'd stolen to Cassie before escorting Uncle Dan to the front door.

"Why does he need a new rig?" Nathan asked.

"I find things. It's what I do, and it doesn't just stop at people or missing items. It apparently extends to oil in the ground. Who knew?" She kicked her leg up and rose with the momentum from Nathan's lap.

Who knew? God forbid if that little secret got out. It wouldn't be a killer Nathan would be hunting down; it would be kidnappers. "You might want to keep that part a secret so I don't have to rescue you from kidnappers."

Her brows furrowed, but she nodded. Men and woman alike down on their luck might be tempted to kidnap someone holding the knowledge of a million-dollar payday if the opportunity arose.

Nathan and Clayton finished eating while Cassie sat on the porch with Nathan's grandfather. He wasn't much of a conversationalist, as he was an observer, but it didn't matter. Nathan could hear the one-sided conversation Cassie was having with the man from inside the house. She was telling him stories about her grandmother's antics.

When they walked outside to let Cassie know they were ready to go to town, there was a certain spark in his granddad's eyes. An all-knowing spark. He really had been amused.

"Ready for me to show you town?" Nathan asked.

"Absolutely." Cassie popped up. "It was nice chatting with you, Mr. Murray."

He lifted his unlit pipe in acknowledgment without saying a word.

"Finally." Clayton groaned. "Maybe I'll meet me a cowgirl or two."

Cassie nudged his shoulder as they crossed the yard heading toward the limo. Nathan headed for his dad's truck.

"I'm driving," Nathan said, holding up the keys.

"Why would we take that? It doesn't even look like it has air conditioning."

Nathan chuckled. "If we take the limo, we won't be blending with the locals or the tourists. We take the truck and go unnoticed. Isn't that the plan?"

"I'm going to need a map," Cassie said. She hopped in the truck like she'd done it a million times then shrugged at his quick gasp. "My sister Faith has a truck older than this one."

"We'll find a map. Maybe this won't take as long as we'd thought."

"You got the bill from the heist?"

Nathan pulled it out of his pocket and handed it to Cassie to hold on to.

Chapter 11

The ride into town was just as bumpy as the ride from the airport, although a lot more scenic. What started out as fields as far as the eye could see turned into houses that were getting closer together until a small metropolis grew before our eyes as if hidden by the horizon and miles of farmland.

Before we reached the town, an indoor arena, flanked by two stables, stood on the outskirts. Horse trailers and big rigs were parked in the gravel lot. Cowboys were carrying bales of hay inside the stables. It was a bigger production than I realized.

"Is that where the competition is going to be?"

"Like clockwork every year. Whoever wins in their divisions ends up representing the state in nationals."

"Let me guess, they get bigger belt buckles as their prizes," Clayton asked.

I nudged Nathan. "You'll have to show me your collection."

His face reddened, making me grin. He was so easy to tease. He probably wouldn't last an entire day around my sisters.

We arrived in the town proper. There were shops and buildings and people milling around. It was more than just a one horse town. There were neighborhoods and schools, along with restaurants and police and fire departments. This part of their town appeared much more like mine. Families shopped on Main Street, and blue and white awnings offered a nice reprieve from the glaring afternoon sun. Kids riding bikes whizzed in and out of traffic. Everybody seemed in a hurry to do their own thing, which I was betting was unusual in this small town if it weren't for the underlying effect that the Benefit and rodeo were just days away.

Nathan parked the truck in front of a sign that read *Cooper's Drug Store*. "If Coop's doesn't have it or can't get it, then it doesn't exist in town."

We all piled out of the truck and headed inside the door. Cool air caressed our faces. This was a hodgepodge-type store. They carried everything from medicines to things you'd see on TV and then some. The store was split into two, sharing space with a western-wear store next door that sold boots and hats.

"His daughter owns the other store," Nathan whispered as he passed. "Come on, if they have what we need, then it will be over here."

I followed behind him, smiling at all the strangers who nodded their head as we passed.

"You and Nathan need to restock, Cassie," Clayton called out from across the store while holding up a box of neon condoms and whipped topping.

I gave him two thumbs-up and smiled. "Get me three of each."

If he thought to embarrass me, then he must not know my sisters very well at all. Red tinted Nathan's cheeks as he paused at the rack of magazines and books.

We scanned each shelf. Nothing, nada.

"My eyes must be deceiving me. Is that Nathan Murray, and is he looking at books?" a woman said as she approached with a big smile on her face. She was a knockout about Nathan's age. Pin-up calendar worthy, blonde hair that hit her waist and big blue eyes. "And here I didn't think you'd ever be coming back to town, much less read."

The woman's gaze went from him to me and back. "I see you brought friends."

I wrapped my arm around Nathan's waist and smiled pretty. "He insisted on bringing me home to meet the folks."

The woman wrinkled her nose. "Is that right, Nathan? Finally slow down long enough to nurture a relationship?"

"Cassie this is Monica Cooper, my ex-girlfriend. Monica, this is Cassie," Nathan said.

"His current girlfriend." I smiled for good measure.

Clayton appeared by my side as if sensing hostility from across the store. He handed me the basket with the neon condoms and the can of Cool Whip. "What did I miss?"

Neither of us spoke.

"The past and the present coming together," Monica answered, holding out her hand. "Cassie, it's a pleasure to meet the woman who snared his heart."

"And you too, Monica, the one who molded him into the man he is."

"I can't take this," Nathan said and strolled off.

"If you ever want to compare notes or do lunch to talk while you're in town, I'm sure I know a few of Nathan's secrets that he hasn't shared."

I grinned. "Nathan secrets sound fun."

"Can I come?" Clayton asked.

Monica turned her gaze to Clayton. She stared at his expensive shoes and then raised her gaze to his gorgeous eyes. "If you play your cards right, Hollywood."

"Is that Nathan Murray, or do my eyes deceive me?" the pharmacist called out from behind the counter. The bald man had a lip full of white whiskers and kind eyes.

"Mr. Cooper, it's good to see you."

I glanced in that direction. "If you'll excuse me. It was a pleasure meeting you."

"You too, Present."

I crossed the store to where Nathan was shaking the pharmacist's hand. "I always hear you've come back to visit but we never see you in town."

"Well, my sister is competing, and then there's the benefit," he answered. "Mr. Cooper, this is Cassie, my girlfriend. Cassie, this is Mr. Cooper."

The pharmacist frowned. "Nathan, I'm guessing you didn't give your girlfriend that black eye, and if you're here for the Domestic Violence Benefit and Ball, does that mean she's a guest speaker?"

I reached for my eye and remembered that I probably looked like hell. "Oh, God, no." I tried for a smile. "No one I loved did this to me. It was a work accident."

Mr. Cooper's gaze went from mine to Nathan's and back again.

"You should find new work."

I gave him a lopsided grin, unwilling to elaborate. "Mr. Cooper, do you have any local maps?"

"Paper maps? Why would you need one of those when you have a native showing you around?"

Nathan's mouth parted, and he snapped it closed.

"I collect them. I know it sounds silly, but I collect them from every place I've been to. It's a keepsake of my travels," I said.

"That's sweet, dear, but I'm afraid they might as well be dinosaur fossils. Nowadays people just use their phones when they want to get places, including old men like me."

I was starting to realize that. I'd tried once to use my crystal with a tablet once, but that didn't work. I couldn't get any accuracy with the read. I think it had something to do with it being electronic that was throwing it off kilter. Regardless, this wasn't looking good.

No map, no scrying. No scrying, no money. No money, no killer.

Chapter 12

He was right. I knew it. My practices were kind of outdated. Nathan, Clayton, and I stepped out into the smoldering Texas heat, where it was hard to breathe. An iridescent shimmer formed on my skin.

"What now?" Nathan asked.

I shrugged. I didn't know. Normally I had time to prepare. Clients sent me their things in advance, and I had time to do whatever I needed. Sometimes I didn't even need a map. The crystal would do all the talking, or visions would just pop into my head and point me in the right direction. Just like my recent case of the keys hidden inside a crockpot.

"We old-school it," I said and glanced up and down the street.

"And what exactly does that mean?" Clayton asked as he and Nathan followed me.

I had my fingers wrapped around the crystal at my neck, trying hard to concentrate on the feelings it was giving off. The strength of the vibration would be my guide. I walked in one direction and then moved back to the store and walked in the other. I grinned and glanced over my shoulder.

"This way. We definitely need to go this way." When they didn't move, I returned to them. "What's the problem?"

"I'm not dressed for this occasion," Clayton mumbled. "I should have worn my tennis shoes."

"Here, take the truck back to the house." Nathan passed him the keys. "I'll call you when we're done."

"Come on. Let's go. I don't want to lose the momentum," I said, already looking back over my shoulder in the direction I wanted to walk.

"You're just going for a walk around town, right? You'll call me when you hit on something so I can come back?" Clayton asked.

Nathan's brows dipped. "Of course, I will."

Clayton left us on the sidewalk, and Nathan tossed his arm around my shoulder. "We're just out for an afternoon stroll to onlookers. You just lead the way."

I didn't have the heart to tell him that his touch sent me into a tizzy. I didn't have the heart to tell him that I wished his words were true.

We took it slow through town, stopping a few times as people approached Nathan. Had I known my way around town, I might have left him so we could get done quicker. I held the bank heist money in one hand and my crystal in the other.

It wasn't until we were standing in front of the bank that any hope I had vanished, and my shoulders deflated.

"Please tell me that isn't the bank where your mom died."

He sighed. "Yep. Maybe the money isn't going to help us after all."

Nathan's Uncle Dan waved as he passed and pulled into the bank parking lot. A man was sitting on the sidewalk in front of the building, resting his head in his palms.

"Do you think he's okay?" I asked.

"My uncle will take care of him." Nathan gestured with his finger toward where his uncle was headed in the young man's direction.

The man rose to his feet. His hands gestured wildly as they exchanged heated words.

"Maybe you should go check on him." I said gesturing to Uncle Dan.

Before Nathan could even cross the street, the man who'd been sitting met our gaze and started slowly started to walk off.

My stomach grumbled as the sun began to set. Our day had been wasted. A dead end.

"Come on. Let's get you something to eat, and then we'll call Clayton to come and pick us up."

I snapped the heist money and held it up. "Too bad we can't use this."

He chuckled and took it from me, stashing it in his pocket. "That would be the quickest way to get the FBI into town."

Nathan took me to this dive of a place. I almost balked at the idea of entering a building that looked like it might fall down around us. There was a neon sign above the entrance that wasn't lit up. Mitchell Brothers BBQ.

"This place might not look like much, but the barbecue is to die for," Nathan said as he pulled the doors open.

The crowd inside was bustling, unlike what I'd expected from the outer appearance. Tables were strategically scattered around the place. Waitresses dressed from head to toe in black were walking around, carrying trays of food to the tables.

Broken peanut shells littered the floor. They crunched beneath our feet as Nathan rested his hand on my back and pointed to a table in the distance near the dance floor.

"Food and dancing?"

"They bring in a DJ on the weekends. We'd have to come back tomorrow if you want me to teach you the two-step. We're lucky to get a table, seeing as they're closing early tonight. Several of their workers are in the rodeo." Nathan chuckled as we approached the table. He pulled out my chair.

The linoleum tabletop shined from the last cleaning.

We hadn't been seated for a minute when Amanda appeared at our table. "Are you following me?"

"What are you doing here, squirt?" Nathan asked as he handed me a menu.

"We're seated across the room." Amanda gestured over her shoulder to a table full of girls.

"Staying out of trouble I hope," Nathan said.

Amanda rested her hand on her jutted hip and raised a brow at her big brother. I'd been there before, just with my big sister instead. There was nothing like having an authority figure watching your every move.

"We're just going to eat and then leave," I reassured her. "Don't worry. I'll make sure he doesn't bother you."

"Thanks, Cassie." She lifted her chin in acknowledgment before spinning around and darting across the room.

A waitress appeared in the next five minutes. We placed our orders, and she returned with our drinks before leaving us again.

"I'm sorry the money led to the bank," I said, reading the disappointment in his eyes. "Maybe the thief took out a safety deposit box to keep the money safe and hidden, or maybe he opened an account with the money that wasn't ruined from the paint explosion."

"If that were the case, that would confirm my suspicion that the robber still alive was local."

I rested my hand over his. He lifted his gaze to mine.

"Don't lose hope. I'm not done yet." I gave him a sad smile.

He took my hand in his and held it. "What more can you do?"

I shrugged. "I have a few ideas still up my sleeve."

Food arrived a short time later, and as promised, the barbeque was to die for, and I'd only had the ribs. They had a full menu of stuff I still needed to try.

"So why did you leave town? Monica seems nice." I held up my hand. "You don't have to answer that; I'm prying, just ignore me."

Nathan's lips twitched as he lifted the beer to his lips. "We were good together. It just turned out we wanted different things. I wanted to leave, and I asked her to come with me. She wanted to stay."

"So, it was geography?" I asked.

"It was more than that, but..." His eyes widened as he stared over my head, making me glance over my shoulder.

A mountain of a man was headed in our direction. Six-foot-something, he would tower over me. His scowl was deeper than any I'd seen on Nathan's face. His cowboy hat had a wide brim, his belt buckle even wider.

"Murray." The mountainous cowboy's voice was deep and threatening.

Chapter 13

Nathan rose and extended his hand. "John."

They shook hands, but the vibes around them were sharp and cold like shards of ice.

I stood and wiped my mouth, holding out my hand to the newcomer. I was on the clock again; my job as a girlfriend was becoming easier. "Hi, I'm Cassie."

"I've heard about you." John looked at my hand and then dismissed it, meeting Nathan's gaze again.

Well, alrighty then. I rested my hand on my hip.

"You're being rude to my girlfriend, John. That's not okay."

John glanced at me again, as if seeing me for the first time. "What are you going to do Nathan, arrest me?"

I huffed out a breath and met John's scowl with my own. "Listen here, you jackass. You're ruining our dinner, so if you don't mind…"

"I do mind," John said and gestured to the door. "Let's take this outside and settle it like men."

"You've got it." Nathan pulled out his wallet and dropped a few bills onto the table.

"You can't really mean to fight in the streets." My whisper was loud as I grabbed my purse and followed behind them. "You're an FBI agent for heaven's sake."

They pushed through the doors and headed around the corner to the alley. They stared death rays at each other. The air was thick with emotion. The stars in the night sky were hidden beneath clouds as if they, too, didn't want to witness this disaster. Lightning flashed in the distance. The two men squared off as I held my breath, debating if there was any way I could stop them from this childish act.

Time seemed to move slowly as they glared at each other, as I waited to see who would make the first punch. Neither of them moved.

"You two knock it off," Monica said as she appeared from behind me. Both men grinned and then laughed as they pulled each other into that manly pat on the back version of a hug.

"You should have told me you were coming to town," John said, nudging his cowboy hat out of his eyes.

"What, and ruin the show you just put on?"

"Wait, I don't understand," I said, holding up my hands in the air.

John took one of my hands and kissed my palm. "Cassie, it's a pleasure to meet you. Monica came home and told me all about you."

My brows dipped as I turned to Nathan.

He blushed as he slid his hands into his jeans pockets. "John and I were best friends. We used to compete against each other, and, well, the stands weren't filling up, so we'd devised a plan to get more people to attend."

"We staged a dislike for each other, fighting over a girl."

Monica waved her fingers. "I was the girl."

"And what started out as fun and games turned into something stronger, didn't it, honey?" John said, pulling Monica into his arms, bending her over his arm, and kissing her senseless.

"So, let me get this straight. You were best friends with Nathan, and you stole his girlfriend?"

"Well, when you put it like that, I sound like an ass."

"What other way is there to put it?" I asked, resting my hands on my hips, seeing these two in a different, very manipulative light.

"Nathan and I had already separated before he'd left town," Monica said, as if explaining.

"And you just stepped in and swept her off her feet?" Cassie growled.

"It's fine, Cass. They belong together," Nathan said, wrapping his arms around my waist. He leaned in and kissed my cheek. "Besides, I stole her from him first."

"Dude, that was first grade and you picked a flower from your mother's prized rose garden and gave it to her. How was I supposed to compete with that?" John said.

"What girl could turn down the prettiest rose this side of the Mississippi after he told me I was just as pretty?" Monica said, leaning into John's chest.

John smiled at Monica before pressing his lips to hers in a kiss that heated *my* cheeks. They broke the embrace, and John whispered, "I love you."

"I love you too, baby," Monica said, wrapping her arm around his waist. "Now feed me before I have to kill you and reconsider my options."

I chuckled. This entire situation was crazy, but I liked Monica. She was as nutty as my family. Not that I'd let her get within ten feet of Nathan. My stomach twisted at the thought.

"You two are coming to the competitions, right?" John asked.

"Aren't you too old to still be competing?" Nathan teased. "I'd hate for you to break a hip." Nathan chuckled.

"I'm not competing anymore. I'm a judge." He held out his hand and shook Nathan's again. "Swing by the house tomorrow afternoon. I'm barbequing."

"Oh, I don't think that's a good idea," Nathan said, backtracking.

Monica took John's hand and started pulling him out of the alley. She pointed at me. "Cassie, you two should show up. I promise embarrassing stories."

I smiled. Nathan dropped his arms from around my waist and took me by the hand.

"That was interesting."

"I would have warned you, but there wasn't time." Nathan glanced at me and grinned.

"You had me fooled."

"John is Uncle Dan's son. Our families used to vacation and rodeo together. They still do sometimes. Amanda and Marty still ride together. They're thick as thieves."

There was no question that Amanda and Marty were close, but I think there was more to their story than just being on the circuit together. When they'd been over, I watched as Amanda's entire demeanor changed from a take-charge type of girl into one a bit shyer as Marty approached. Not that I'd mention that to Nathan.

"So where to now?" I asked.

Nathan led me up the street. "I need to make one more stop if that's okay with you."

The streets were deserted this time of night. We walked hand in hand almost to the outskirts of town near where the rodeo was set up. He turned at a brick sign that read, Millville Cemetery.

'You know I've had dates take me to a lot of unusual places, but the cemetery is a first for me."

Nathan chuckled. "You aren't scared, are you?"

"Ghosts and zombies don't scare me," I teased and forced myself not to rub at the goosebumps forming on my arm. I wasn't lying. Those things didn't scare me; it was the thought of being buried alive. My sister Mercy had touched me once and made the mistake of telling me how I was going to die. At the time we were young and it was just a game. It was soon after we realized that she'd accurately predicted other deaths.

So now, I stayed clear of places where those things might come to pass. I fought hard to control my thoughts from straying and making it worse. I watched my step as we walked. I scanned my surrounding. There wasn't a threat in sight. No yawning pit for me to fall into, no skulking villain lurking nearby to make that happen.

Tension knotted in my shoulders as Nathan stopped at a grave. Jenna Murray was carved into the stone's surface. Roses sat in the attached vase. She'd been forty-three when she died and had died on her birthday.

"How awful that she died on her birthday. That must make celebrating her life more difficult since you mourn her too."

"She was still in her prime," Nathan said, lowering to his knees. He picked the stray leaves resting at the bottom of the stone and tossed them away. "Every year on her birthday my dad would buy her a cake and Mildred would help me make some dried pasta necklace or something as equally stupid, and my mom would disappear for two hours of her birthday without fail. My dad used to tell me that she deserved it. It was her *me-time*."

"She was probably going to the spa or getting her nails done," I offered.

Nathan chuckled. "Mom didn't bother with her nails. They stayed dirty digging in her flower gardens. She used to tell me the more time she spent with her flowers, the more peace of mind they gave her."

Flowers made her calm? If that was the case, maybe I should try something similar.

I ran my fingers over the beautiful petals. The crystal vibrated against my chest. Maybe there was something to this. Maybe his mother had solved how to de-stress. "Maybe I should try to grow a garden."

Nathan pulled dimes from his pocket and used his finger to dig a tiny hole next to her headstone. He placed them in the hole and covered them up.

"Are you trying to grow a money tree, because, let me tell you, I've tried. It didn't work."

"I always leave her dimes. She likes to put them in my path."

"You know they check in on us, right? One of my sisters is like a ghost whisperer."

Chapter 14

"She would have liked you, you know." Nathan's rested his palm on my cheek in a tender caress. His gaze softened as we sat in the grass beneath the Texas sky. He leaned in. His breath was hot against my mouth as he stared into my eyes. "Thank you for helping me."

He pressed his lips to mine in a heated kiss making my heartbeat quicken. His lips were warm and moist, sending shivers of desire down my body to places long neglected. My body responded to his touch and eagerly responded to his kiss.

His gentle lips caressed mine until he pulled away, resting his forehead against mine. Our heated breaths mingled and matched in intensity.

"Why did you stop?" I asked.

"I don't want to take advantage of you."

I rested my palm around his neck and pulled him close to whisper against his lips. "You make me feel alive, and I haven't felt that in a long time. I'm ready to explore this, whatever it is."

Gone was the gentle kiss, replaced by something more akin to desire and demand. He covered my mouth and pulled me into his arms so, when I felt something hard against my head, it took a minute to pull out of the sexual haze I'd been heading into. I broke the kiss abruptly, leaving the warmth of his hold and his mouth.

"Give me your money," a man growled as he yanked me to my feet, holding the gun to my head.

Nathan stared up at us, about to stand. "Stay right where you are and empty out your pockets, or she dies."

Nathan's eyes narrowed.

There was a desperation in this man's voice as his fingers bit punishingly into my arm. It took me only a second to realize I recognized him. The man from the bank was holding me at gunpoint.

"Here," I said, offering my purse. "Take whatever's in there."

He cocked the trigger and gestured toward Nathan. "Throw it to him so he can add in his cash. I know he has money. I saw you two at the bank."

I tossed Nathan my purse. He slowly slid his wallet out of his pocket and pulled out the cash. "I'm afraid you only get the cash; I won't give up the badge."

The man's grip on me tightened at his newfound realization.

"No one has to get hurt." Nathan showed that each of the compartments was empty but his ID. "Let her go."

"Your phone, too, and empty out your pockets." He gestured with the gun then pressed it harder into my temple.

Nathan held out his hand as if to still the robber's actions. "Okay, okay."

Nathan pulled out his phone and shoved it into my purse before pulling out the tainted hundred-dollar bill from the heist. He yanked open the evidence bag and took the bill out. The evidence bag fluttered to the ground as Nathan shoved the bill into my purse.

He tossed it at my feet. The tension in the air was thick.

"Pick it up." The robber kept his gaze on Nathan while holding the gun to my head as I slowly bent to retrieve my purse.

"Let her go."

The man tsked. "She's my ticket out of here. You stay put, and no harm will come to her. If I even think that you're following us, I'll kill her."

"What guarantees do we have that you're not going to kill her anyway?" Nathan asked, slowly rising to his feet.

"If that were the case, I'd shoot you first and kill you both. Are you sure you want to test my word?"

"It's fine," I pleaded with Nathan. "I'm fine, Nathan. He hasn't hurt me, and I don't think he will."

The man wrapped his arm around my chest and started walking us backward into the darkness of night. He called out as we moved between headstones. "Stay put, or she dies."

I almost tripped, and he had to stop me from falling. "Sorry."

"Don't try anything funny," he said as his hold on me tightened, his hand pressed hard against the crystal at my neck. We were almost at a backward run when he stopped and turned me in his arms.

My breath caught. He'd stopped us at an empty hole already dug in the ground.

He yanked the pendant from my neck and gestured with the gun. "In the hole. I can't afford you chasing me."

I slowly shook my head. "I'm claustrophobic. Please don't. I promise not to chase you."

Confusion and a hint of concern crossed his face before it was masked. I dropped to my knees. "I'll stay right here. I promise."

He shook his head and pointed toward the hole again. "Get in."

Just when I thought he was going to have to kill me to get in the hole, I realized I was wrong. A single gunshot near my feet had done the trick.

I slid down into the hole and pressed my back to the farthest end.

"Your boyfriend will come to save you, and if he doesn't, I'll send someone else."

That confession confused me. I didn't care if what he said was true as long as the next bullet wasn't in my body.

The man tore off in a run without looking back.

I was stuck in a dirt hole, but he hadn't killed me, but he might as well have. My hand landed on my bare neck. That crystal wasn't just for decoration, and it didn't just help me find people and things. It helped keep my energy grounded.

"One problem at a time," I whispered out loud to whatever worms wriggled nearby.

"Cassie." Nathan's yell came from a distance as I tried not once, but twice to find a hold in the side of the packed dirt.

"Nathan," I yelled back, trying to climb out, but I fell onto my butt.

"Cassie." His yell was getting louder.

"I'm in a large hole," I yelled back.

Nathan found me minutes later, and I'd never been so happy to see his face.

"Thank God. I thought he shot you." Relief flooded his face. "Are you hurt?" He lay down on the ground and held out his hands for me to grab.

"Only my pride that I can't get myself out of here," I said, taking his outstretched hands. He pulled me out and held me in his embrace.

"Are you okay? Did he hurt you?"

"No, and when I told him I was claustrophobic, he said the weirdest thing. He said if you didn't find me, he'd make sure someone came back to pull me out," I answered, rubbing the dirt off my butt.

"A robber with a conscience. That's a first."

"He didn't take your badge either, Nathan."

"The man held you at gunpoint, Cassie. Tell me you aren't taking pity on him."

"No, I'm just saying, who in their right mind would leave an FBI agent alive if he stole all the money? He has to know his time is limited before you find him."

"Let's agree to disagree," he said as he took my hand.

"Any chance there's a pay phone nearby where we can call your house collect so someone can come get us?"

"There hasn't been a pay phone around here in a decade, and all of the shops are closed. We're stuck out here until morning."

"I'm not sleeping in a cemetery, especially the one we just got robbed in."

Nathan glanced in my direction. His mouth tilted up in the corner. "I know the perfect place where we'll be safe and undisturbed to get some sleep until daybreak."

Thirty minutes later, after walking for a mile, Nathan led me into the stables at the fairgrounds. He walked in like he'd been there plenty of times and knew where to go. He stopped in front of a gate and opened it. Nathan's last name was written on paper and hung outside the empty stall. Hay filled the area.

"Is this your home away from home?" I asked and gestured to the name.

He chuckled. "Not mine, but Amanda's. This spot is reserved for her horse."

Chapter 15

"Nathan, I need my…" My words died on my lips as Nathan crushed his lips to mine.

He eased the kiss to whisper, "If you'd gotten hurt, I never would have forgiven myself for dragging you down here."

"You talk too much," I whispered and took over the kiss, a warm slide of our tongues as he pulled me closer. He gathered me into his arms and gently laid me on the hay, following me down. His hands caressed my body. I don't know if it was the adrenaline we were both swimming in or something else, but I didn't just want him; I needed him.

His warm palms sent tingles down my spine as they rested, touching skin just below the hem of my shirt.

"We shouldn't…" he said, breaking the kiss.

"We are," I answered, resuming the kiss, only this time moving his entire palm to touch my stomach skin to skin.

As if that little contact lit a fire beneath him, his lips left mine, kissing a trail down my neck as his hand lifted my shirt and landed on my bra. He leaned over me and lowered my bra with his teeth, sending shockwaves through my body.

My heartbeat raced as I watched him take my nipple into his mouth. My head dropped back, and I moaned, lifting my body into his. I needed to feel him. I needed his hands and mouth all over me. My body was on fire and in a sexual haze of need.

He'd finished with the right one and then worked his way to the other as I pulled the shirt over my head. His fingers toyed with the button of my jeans as I grabbed his shirt at the shoulder blades and pulled his off too.

In a hurried state now, the rest of our clothes came off within minutes. He was poised at the juncture of my thighs.

He paused. "I don't have a condom, but I'm clean."

"Me too, and I'm on the pill," I whispered, taking his lips again.

He eased into me, slowly until seated to the hilt. The hay poking my skin was forgotten. He stared down at me with heat in his eyes. "Are you okay?"

"I will be when you get moving, cowboy." I grinned, nudging him with my heels.

It wasn't long before he took us both over the edge. He grunted my name when we both found our release.

We lay unmoving, a twisted pile of limbs. Our chests rose and fell in rhythm. "That was... whoa." He let out a breath.

"Amazingly hot," I answered. "Next time I'll wear nothing but cowboy boots and a grin."

He rolled over me and pressed a tender kiss to my lips. His warm palm lay heavy on my stomach. "Next time I'll hold you to that, and it will be in a bed."

I chuckled as he pushed up from his spot. I took my time drinking in his amazing body. Heat flushed my cheeks from thoughts of wanting him again.

He slid first his boxers and then his jeans up his long powerful legs before fastening them at the waist. "Wait here, and I'll go find something to clean us up. I know where they keep their supplies."

He gave me a salacious wink before he slipped out of the stall, returning a few minutes later with towels to clean away the evidence of our hot and dirty deed. I slid back into my clothes and lay in his arms.

"Get a few hours' sleep. The crews will come in early, and I'll borrow a phone and get us a ride back to the ranch."

My eyes were already closing. The night was nothing like I'd expected, but I settled into the warmth of the crook of his arm. My palm rested over his heart, and I proceeded to fall asleep.

I was dreaming. I knew I was. In the dream I sat next to a fire, the subconscious flames hot on my cheeks. My sister Talia and my parents were on the other side of the firepit. It could have been a memory of our last camping trip. I eased my seat back, and it was as though the flame was following.

Panic raced my heart, and my eyes flew open.

"Nathan," I whispered.

We were no longer in the stall but in his bedroom. Sheets covered my body while an icepack rested on my forehead.

"Cassie," he answered and hurried to my side, dropping to his knees. Dark stubble outlined his strong jaw, and his hair was mussed, as if he'd raked his fingers through it repeatedly. "I thought I'd lost you twice."

"What happened?" I asked, my throat dry and scratchy.

"We fell asleep in the stall, and when I woke up, you were burning up with a fever and unresponsive. I got you back here, and Mildred and I have been watching out for you. It wasn't until Clayton called Gwen to explain what was going on that she told us what to do."

My brows dipped, my thoughts twisting in turmoil. It was like he wasn't making any sense.

"I don't understand."

"You remember the robber, right?" he asked.

I nodded.

"I didn't know anything about your crystal until Gwen asked if you still had your necklace. When I checked, you didn't. The robber took your crystal." He pressed a tender kiss to my lips.

"I need my crystal. It helps keep my energy grounded."

"That's an understatement, child," Mildred said from across the room. "We thought you'd been possessed when we got you here. There were mirrors breaking and glasses too. We didn't know what the hell was going on."

"If my tapped energy isn't controlled, the vibration has been known to give me a fever and break things nearby." It had only happened once before. Once I'd almost died. Once had been enough to learn that lesson.

"Your sister told me any crystal would help you, so that's why you've got the crystal from the chandelier hanging from your neck. Sorry about the fishing line. It was all we had from when Nathan used to make his momma those sweet necklaces."

I reached for the crystal and held it up. A smile split my lips. "I should start carrying more than one in the event that ever happens again."

"I should say so," Mildred answered as Nathan stared down at me.

I tried to sit up, and Nathan helped. "How long have I been out?"

"Two days." He held the glass of water to my lips. "Clayton has been giving your sister updates. She threatened to bring all of your sisters here if you weren't awake in the next six hours."

"That's a scary thought."

He sat down on the bed beside me and leaned in to kiss me again. His gaze was soft, his hold strong.

"Let that girl breathe, Nathan."

Nathan pulled away but held my gaze. "I made a police report. They're looking for our robber, and I also had to call it into the FBI since he took the heist evidence. I'll probably be reprimanded for that."

"I'm sorry, Nathan," I whispered. "Let me get dressed, and we'll go search for him."

"You aren't going anywhere, child," Mildred announced. "I'm going to make you a sandwich and some soup. When you can keep that down, and your fever is one hundred percent gone, then you can think about going out and about."

"But…"

"She's right," Nathan added. "Regain your strength first."

An hour later, I was sitting on the porch with Nathan's grandfather and Clayton. He'd given a slight nod as I took a seat, as if to welcome me back to the land of the living without spending any precious words.

A late afternoon breeze caressed my face as Amanda ran out to the barn where her horse was corralled. The workers at the first oil rig were in the distance, taking a break and sitting in the shade while other machinery men had started to stabilize the digging equipment in another area on the property.

"That didn't take long to get the equipment."

"Feel free to tell me the lottery numbers or where diamonds are hidden," Clayton said, jostling my arm. We slowly rocked on the swing as if this was exactly where we belonged.

"I'll be sure to let you know."

"So." Clayton clapped his hands. "You didn't have any luck with the money, and you were robbed, so when are we blowing this joint?"

I shrugged, unsure how to answer. I wasn't in any hurry to go back, not with the niggling feeling that this wasn't quite over. "You don't have to stay and babysit me. I'll be fine."

"Yeah, like when I left you alone for a minute, and you not only got robbed but developed a life-threatening fever? You mean, fine like that?"

I nudged his arm back as Amanda came running across the yard. She ran right into her dad as he and Nathan opened the screen door.

"Where's the fire, Amanda?" his dad asked.

"I lost Mom's good luck pin that I clip onto the saddle before every competition. If I don't find it, I'm not going to win."

"Where did you see it last?" he asked.

"The barn, but it might have fallen off when I took Obi out on one of our morning rides. It could be anywhere."

A look of despair fell across Amanda's face as if her entire world was crumbling. Tears welled up in her eyes. I rose. "I'll help you find it since I haven't had much luck with anything else."

Amanda swiped a fallen tear. "You will?"

"Of course, but you need to take me to the barn."

"Cassie, you don't have to—"

"Yeah, I do." I smiled and headed off the porch.

Nathan rested his palm on my arm as I passed. He cupped my cheek and leaned in to kiss me. It was quick and gentle, but I got the message. Nathan had just announced to everyone watching that we were an actual item, and not just pretend. Everyone who mattered would read how real that kiss had been. "Stay out of trouble and holler if you need any help."

"No need," Clayton said as he rose off the swing. "I'll go with them so Gwen doesn't think I'm just here enjoying the scenery, as she so aptly put it."

"My sister wouldn't know a good time if it were to sneak up and bite her in the...well, never mind," I said, heading down the steps.

Chapter 16

I couldn't find anything else we'd been looking for, so maybe helping to find this good luck charm would dust the cobwebs off and rev things up again. If nothing else, it would give this new crystal trinket around my neck a good workout.

We entered the barn, where more than the one horse was stabled; there were two. One I'd yet to see Amanda ride. This barn was nothing like the one Nathan and I had slept in. That one had several stalls and locked boxes and other things. This one had hay stacked against the back wall going up to the second-story loft area.

"What's up there?" I asked.

"Oh, just a bed and blankets. Sometimes the oil roughnecks will bunk here, especially if they work into the night."

"Which horse is yours?"

Amanda opened the stall door and rubbed the horse's neck. "This is Obi-Wan."

I grinned at the name as I rubbed the horse's nose.

"You must like *Star Wars*."

"My brother named him. Obi was his horse before he gave him to me."

"Where do you normally keep the pin?"

"On Obi's saddle," Amanda answered, closing the stall. She crossed the barn to where several saddles sat astride a bench. Just ready to be picked up and lain on the back of the horse. Amanda pointed to the one closest to us.

The leather was faded, cracked, and embellished with several swirls and etches carved into the leather around the seat. "How is it you connect it onto the saddle. I would think the leather would break the pin."

"Oh, right," Amanda said. "I attach it to Obi's blanket."

Amanda walked across the room to where several blankets were folded. She handed me the one on top. I picked it up and inhaled, trying to get a bead on what might have happened.

I didn't even need to open my senses to figure it out. A simple sniff told me everything. "This was laundered recently."

"Once a week if not more, but always before competitions," Amanda said, her eyes widening as if just saying the words out loud activated her brain cells again.

"Go check. We'll wait here in case we're wrong."

Amanda ran from the barn, yelling for Mildred on her way.

"Where is she going?" Clayton asked.

"To check the washer and dryer." I handed him the blanket. "It smells fresh and clean."

I picked up the one beneath it and instantly pictured an image of Amanda and Marty. They were lying atop of it and kissing by a lake I'd yet to explore.

Amanda came running back a few minutes later, holding up the pin. "You were right."

"Case solved." Clayton rubbed his hands together.

"Can you give us a minute?" I asked Clayton with a nod toward the door.

"Sure, I'll be on the porch."

I waited until he was gone and Amanda had gotten busy re-pinning the good luck charm to the blanket.

I held up the other blanket. "You know, when I was younger, there was this boy that I crushed on something fierce. I would have given him anything. I would have done anything, so imagine my surprise when he showed interest in me. I ate it up without question. One thing led to another, and well, I wish I could take back what I gave him and saved it for someone more special."

Amanda's brows dipped as she turned to look at me. I handed her the blanket. "The river has kept your secret, and I will, too, but if you ever need to talk, you can call me."

Realization dawned on her face as she clutched that blanket to her chest. "I love Marty. He gets me."

I smiled at her. I could only hope that he loved her back and her heart didn't get crushed like mine had at her age.

"Like I said, if you ever need to talk, you can call me. I've been there and done that. I know you have Mildred, but still. I have sisters, and we've been there for each other. Just consider me the same. If you ever need anything."

"Thanks, Cassie," she said as a look of relief crossed her face. "When my mom died, I didn't realize how much I'd miss her. How much I'd need her. Dad tries, and Nathan does too, but there are just some things they don't understand." Amanda was a young and beautiful eighteen-year-old. There was a light in her eyes and a fire in her heart at her zest for life.

"Sweetie, sometimes even age doesn't change that."

We walked out of the barn and back to the house. I hadn't had to use my crystal to find the trinket, so I had yet to determine if it would work. I needed practice. I needed to know if this crystal could encase my energy and work to stabilize me, or I'd be in a boatload of uncertainty.

Nathan was waiting for me on the porch while everyone else had disappeared. Amanda jogged passed him and patted his arm. "I like this one. You should keep her."

His brows rose, and I chuckled. "I offered girl-talk."

Nathan pulled me into his arms and stared down into my eyes. "You know you've opened a can of worms. She's not a typical girly girl."

"Maybe not, but she still has crushes and boyfriends."

Nathan plugged his ears. "I don't need to hear anymore."

"Funny," I said, opening the screen door. "Do you still have the evidence bag that the money was in?"

"Yeah." Nathan's uncertainty was clear.

"I need to test out this crystal. I didn't need it to find the pin. I used my powers of deduction." I climbed the stairs.

Nathan rested his palm on my arm, stopping me in my tracks. "You want to see if you can track the stolen bill back using the bag."

"That's the plan. The money has been sitting in that bag for over a week. That should have been enough contact for me track that single hundred-dollar bill to its current location." I gave him a quick smile. The bag wouldn't take us to the heist money, but it should take us directly to the guy who'd robbed us and right now that was all we needed. "I need to test this crystal and find my other one and that money. Only this time, we won't be caught off guard." I raised my brows. "So, you, Mr. Murray, need to keep your hands to yourself."

I spun around and jogged up the stairs.

"Easier said than done," Nathan said from behind. I glanced over my shoulder to find his gaze glued to my backside.

"You do have an extra gun or two hanging around, right?" I asked.

"You aren't getting a gun, but you will go armed," he answered, walking past me.

We headed up to the third floor.

"You should have named the horse Yoda because you're talking in riddles."

He knocked on a bedroom door. The sign hung that read, Keep Out. "Amanda's room?"

"Come in," she yelled through the closed door.

He twisted the knob and opened the door, taking a step into the room.

Amanda had her cell phone pressed against her ear.

"I need to borrow your stun gun, squirt."

"I'll call you back," she whispered into the phone and hung up. "Why do you need my stun gun? Did you forget where you hid your bullets?"

"It's not for me; it's for Cassie. We're going hunting."

"And you want to kill Bambi with a stun gun?" she asked. "That's just wrong on so many levels."

"We're hunting robbers," I corrected as Amanda handed me the pink-stone-embellished stun gun.

"Oh well then, hooyah, go get 'em, and happy hunting," Amanda said, holding on to the doorknob in a not-so-subtle way of telling us to get lost.

Chapter 17

Nathan borrowed Mildred's four-door sedan in an attempt to be less conspicuous. We'd driven up and down each street, and I'd held on to the crystal in one hand and the evidence bag in the other. I could feel the tingling as we neared even without a vision of where the property was.

It vibrated hard in my hand as we neared the library. I rested my hand on Nathan's arm. "Stop here."

He did, and I climbed out with him following behind.

He walked with me up the street before I turned back around and walked to the car. I glanced up and down the street, only taking a step in each different direction until I stared up at the library.

The red brick building was dark. A closed sign was hung on the door. There was nothing suspicious. Maybe my wires had gotten crossed.

"Let's check it out," Nathan said as he took my hand and led me down the alleyway. The building next to the library was the historical society. Those windows were dark too.

We crept down the alley, Nathan releasing my hand as we neared the end of the building.

The movement of the crystal vibration prodded me to go running around. I could feel it; we were near, and that meant trouble. I pulled out the stun gun and waited with my finger on the trigger as Nathan peered from around the corner.

He nodded and held his finger to his lips.

I stepped around him and peered with him. The man that had robbed us was carrying a basket filled with fruit as he pulled open the door to a storm shelter. He gave one look around before he was about to descend the steps.

Nathan sprang like a tiger and held his gun to the man's head. "You don't get to disappear this time."

The man stood stock-still. His gaze widened as I approached.

He had fresh peaches, apples, and a slew of other fruits and veggies in his hands.

"Daddy, I'm hungry," a small voice called out from the darkness below as he stepped into the light.

The man slowly lowered the basket of food to the ground and held up his hands. "Arrest me, but don't hurt my kids."

"What is this place?" I asked, stepping around them both. I eased down the stairs before Nathan could stop me.

"Cassie, get back here," Nathan growled as I reached the last step.

Light danced shadows off the brick walls. There was a group of people, fifteen without counting the kids sitting on blankets on the floor.

"We don't want any trouble," a woman whispered. "Please, just leave."

"I can't do that," I said as I moved farther into the room, stepping through the maze of people. With each step I took, I could feel the draw and knew I was closer. I opened an ancient-looking cabinet. My purse was nestled inside. The money from my wallet was gone, but the credit cards, ID, and crystal were perched on a shelf inside the cabinet.

"Thank God," I said, pulling it free. I slid it around my neck and grabbed our things, including the ruined hundred-dollar bill. There was a stack of identical red-dyed hundred-dollar bills sitting next to it.

"Nathan, you need to get down here," I called out.

A child across the room moaned and violently coughed. I took a step in that direction out of habit, and a woman pulled a little girl against her chest and rubbed her back. "It's just a bad cough."

Nathan stepped into the room with the man in handcuffs. He eased him to sit on his butt in the corner of the room as he gauged the current threat.

"Nathan Murray, when did you get back into town?" a man asked, stepping out of the shadow. He held his weathered cowboy hat against his dirty clothes.

"Pastor Bigsby?" Nathan asked.

The man stepped forward and shook Nathan's hand.

"Pastor?" I asked.

"These are good people, Nathan. They're God's children, just like you, but they fell on hard times. We all did."

"So, let me guess, you send a scout out every night to rob people?" Nathan turned his glare on the man in cuffs.

"No, son. We don't do that. We take what's given to us."

"He didn't ask. He held us at gunpoint," Nathan said, gesturing to the man on the ground.

"Michael, what have you done?"

"I didn't hurt them, Pastor. Neither of them. I just needed some money for Mary since the bills covered in red wouldn't work."

"His daughter," the pastor clarified and gestured to the kid that had been coughing.

"I've made a list of everything I took. I planned to pay everyone back," Michael, the handcuffed man, whispered in the dark.

Nathan's scowl grew in intensity, and I rested my palm on his arm. "We understand."

"No, we don't," Nathan growled.

"You're all homeless, right?"

"That's not an excuse for breaking the law, Cassie," Nathan said as he glanced around the room.

"Yes, ma'am. The bank called our mortgages, and we couldn't pay. It included the one on my home, or these people would be living there," the pastor announced.

My heart shattered into a million little pieces as I glanced around the room. These people had dirt covering the faces, their clothes were old and in need of repair. Jugs of water sat in the corner. Each person had a piece of fruit or vegetable they'd been coveting.

"How long have you been like this?"

"Three months," the man sitting in handcuffs answered.

Nathan finally lowered his gun. "Our town has resources. Why didn't you go to the city?"

The pastor dropped his head. "The resources were used up. These good people aren't the first that lost everything to the bank."

"I don't understand," Nathan said, and his brows dipped. "Uncle Dan would have helped you."

The man wearing handcuffs tsked. "That no good piece of—"

"Michael, there are children present," the woman clipped from across the room, shuffling the sick girl in her arms.

I touched Nathan's arm and gestured to the cabinet. "You need to go take a look at what Michael has hidden inside."

He walked off while I jogged up the stairs and carried the basket of food to the others. I laid it at the pastor's feet before moving next to the woman with the sick child.

"What's her name?"

"Mary Ellen," the woman answered with a smile.

"What did the doctor say?"

Mary Ellen held up two prescriptions in her hand. "She has a respiratory infection, and he gave us these."

I took them and looked at the scripts. "Why didn't you get those filled?"

"No money," Michael answered from across the room. "We could barely afford the doctor bill with the money I took from you."

"You told me you found it, Michael. What good is it going to do us if you're in jail?" the woman asked.

"Janet, I'd do anything for Mary."

"Not if you are behind bars. Now apologize to these people."

"An apology isn't going to help," Nathan said, turning with the new hundred-dollar bills in his hands. "But telling me everything you know about this might."

"I found those," Michael blurted out. "Had I known they were useless; I wouldn't have tried to use them. I would have left them in the gutter where I found them."

"Gutter?" he asked.

Michael shook his head. "I'm not saying another word unless you promise not to press charges for robbing you."

Tension thickened in the air. Nathan had tipped his hand, and they were at an impasse.

"Nathan, give me your keys."

Nathan tossed me his keys. "Where are you going?

"I'm going to take Janet to the all-night pharmacy and get these prescriptions filled, and then I'm going to go rent some hotel rooms for these people."

His mouth parted. "We're kind of in the middle of something here."

"You are," I answered.

"There won't be any rooms," the Pastor answered. "Not with the competition that kicks off this weekend."

I looked around the room at these kind faces. "We'll figure something out. I promise."

"Why would you help us?" an older gray-haired woman asked from across the room.

"Because it's the right thing to do," I answered as I held back the tears that had gathered in my eyes. I wouldn't cry in front of these people, but I would when I was alone. My heart was breaking, and no way could I just walk away knowing what I knew. No way would my conscience let me.

"I don't have a car seat. Can we leave Mary with someone?"

Janet nodded and crossed the room, handing her daughter to the other older woman. "Momma, you take care of her, and I'll be back soon."

Chapter 18

I drove across town to the all-night pharmacy with Janet pointing out the directions. She reluctantly got out of the car with me. Pink tinted her cheeks as she ran her hand over her clothes, as if trying to hide her appearance.

We walked inside, and I led her toward the back of the store, past all of the people giving us weird looks, and straight into the bathroom.

"You can wash your face and hands if it will make you feel better. I'm going to step out and see if they have any clean clothes."

"You don't have to do that. I just need medicine for my daughter."

I rested my hand on Janet's arm. "Let me do this for you and your daughter."

She reluctantly nodded, and I left her just as she turned the water on in the sink.

I stepped out and hit the tourist aisle in search of T-shirts and lounge pants. The pharmacy was equipped with everything a tourist might need. I grabbed a few items, including some hand wipes, and took them to the register and paid, handing over my credit card.

I signed, and when the cashier went to put the items in the bag, I stopped her. "That's not necessary."

I pulled the tags free and dropped them in the bag and carried all the items into the bathroom, where Janet took her time cleaning herself and changing into clothes.

"We weren't always like this," she said from behind the closed bathroom stall door while I sat on the sink, dangling my legs over the counter.

"What happened, if you don't mind me asking?"

"Our crop got ruined, and we were having a hard time making ends meet, and then things turned worse when the cattle somehow got out and disappeared. It was as if we were struck by bad luck, and it all started when some developers showed up in town wanting to buy our land."

"You think they sabotaged things?" I asked.

"I don't know." Janet appeared from behind the closed door. She ran her fingers through her hair, trying to comb the knots free. "I would hope not, but it was soon after that we missed some payments, and the bank came calling in our mortgage note. We weren't the only ones, either."

"Is that when Michael started stealing?"

"He didn't always steal. He'd come home with fresh fruit and vegetables our old neighbors and friends supplied him with. They didn't mind if he took from their fields. Then he filled water from faucets. He didn't take much, just enough to try and support us to get by. But when Mary got sick, I think that must have scared him into stealing from you. I'm so sorry he did that."

"Desperate times call for desperate measures. If it had been any of my sisters and we were in the same predicament, I might have done the same."

"No, you wouldn't," she answered. "You have a kind soul." Janet put her dirty clothes in the bag, and we gave the pharmacist her script to fill. We were told it would be forty-five minutes, so we walked across the street, and I fed her hamburgers and French fries too. She scarfed them down, trying not to look like a woman on the verge of starvation.

"We'll get some to go and take it to the others. When was the last time you had a decent meal?" I asked.

She shrugged. "We've been surviving on fruit and vegetables, so I can't complain. Homeless people in bigger cities wouldn't even have that to eat."

A plan started forming in my head. It took hold of my heart and wouldn't let go. "I'm going to help you and all of the others. I just need a little time to get my plan into action."

"You aren't a local. Won't you leave after the competition?"

"I'm not here for the competition." I smiled. "I was trying to help Nathan locate some missing items, but I failed."

"Why is that?" she asked while taking a sip of her chocolate milkshake to wash down her French fries.

"I needed a map, and this town doesn't believe in street maps when cell phones are so handy."

Janet swallowed hard. "Why not just go to the property appraiser's office? I've had to go there a bunch checking boundary lines and deeds."

Why in the world hadn't I thought of that? A smile formed on my lips. "Thanks, I'll do that."

"My momma used to work there before she retired. That's how she knew every city office building in town had storm shelters. She still had a key to get in," Janet said.

I bought the store out of all their blankets, wet wipes, toiletries, and everything else I could think of that these people might need. I'd ordered a ton of food and picked it up before returning to the library.

Nathan still hadn't gotten anything useful from Michael by the time we'd unloaded all of our goodies. Both just pure stubbornness.

"Take his cuffs off. He needs to eat," I said.

"Cassie, I'm not removing his handcuffs."

I rested my hand on my hip. "He's malnourished, he was trying to help his baby girl, and he needed money. Can't you just for once give the guy a break?"

"And if Michael does it again and then someone gets hurt?" Nathan asked.

"He won't. Will you, Michael?" I asked, unwrapping a burger.

"I won't. I'll figure something else out, I promise."

"See." Cassie smiled. "He won't do it again, and if he does, then you know where to look." I held the burger up to his mouth, and he took a bite. "If not for me, do it for Janet and Mary, please."

Nathan sighed, rubbing at his temple and held up the hundred-dollar bills. "Why should I give him a break when he won't tell me about the bills?"

"Nathan has a point," I said, holding a drink cup up to Michael's mouth. "Quid pro quo. You should tell him what you know if he promises to drop the charges and not haul you in."

"Does he?" Michael turned to Nathan.

"Do you?"

"Fine." Nathan sighed. "But it better be worth it."

"I found them in a New Orleans gutter."

Nathan's brow rose. "If you're homeless, what were you doing in New Orleans?"

"I found work as a ranch hand, and there was a competition two weeks ago. I traveled with the horse."

Nathan unlocked Michael's restraints, and I handed him the burger, which he scarfed down. I handed him three more.

"And the money was just lying in the gutter?"

Michael nodded. "Right next to the dead body. I made an anonymous call to the police."

"Not before you took some of the money though, right?"

"What was the dead guy going to do with it? He couldn't spend it," Michael said.

"How much was there?" Nathan asked.

"I don't know how much, but it was a pile of it that was painted. I didn't stick around in case the killer decided to return and finish him off with that knife sticking out of his heart."

"Knife?" Nathan asked. "There wasn't a murder weapon left behind."

Michael wiped his mouth with the back of his hand. "I saw it with my own two eyes. It was one of those hunting knives, like in the window over at Carver's Outdoor store."

"That should be easy for you to check if you call the medical examiner. He can probably tell you exactly how Herbert died and they'll be happy to hear that you got your evidence back and added to it."

Nathan took my arm and led me to the other side of the room. "And exactly how am I supposed to explain that I caught the guy and then let him go?"

"You could say you found it. That's not lying. We did find it."

Nathan pointed at Michael. "Don't leave town. I'll have some more questions tomorrow for you."

Michael crossed the room to Mary and picked her up, kissing her head. "I wouldn't leave my family."

"Come on, take me home," I said, guiding Nathan to the stairs. I glanced back one last time. My heart ached to help these people. In that moment, nothing else mattered.

Nathan
Chapter 19

"You could have gotten hurt going into a basement when you had no idea what was down there," Nathan called into the bathroom where Cassie was getting ready for bed.

His heart had jumped out of his chest when she disappeared into the darkness. Any number of things could have happened to her.

"There were hungry kids down there. What did you expect me to do?" she asked.

Nathan rested his hands behind his head and let out a hefty sigh. "Be more vigilant, and start thinking about your own safety."

Cassie stepped out of the bathroom and turned off the light. She was wearing a pair of boy shorts and a tank top that left little to the imagination, and he hardened instantly. Sleeping with her in the horse stall seemed like months ago, and he was hungry for more.

"I can take care of myself, Nathan, or did you forget that I track criminals for a living?"

Nathan reached for her as she climbed onto the bed. He pulled her into his arms and gave her a heated kiss.

She moaned against his lips as she leaned over him. She broke the kiss, determination and fire flickering in her eyes. "I'm going to help those people."

"I believe you," he whispered.

She gave a hard nod before she kissed him again. Nathan rolled until he had her beneath him. He took his time, devouring her and showing her new heights until she lay in a heap of boneless bliss, sound asleep in his arms.

****

The sun was streaming through the windows into the room. The warmth of the rays woke Nathan from a sound sleep. He glanced to the bed next to him to find Cassie already gone. Scrubbing his hand down his face, he tossed the covers aside and got out of bed. After tugging on some jeans, he walked to the window to find his dad and Cassie standing around the new oil rig.

A smile formed at the corner of his mouth. Cassie was clapping and jumping up and down and had thrown her arms around Nathan's dad's neck. "I guess they struck black gold."

"It's a gusher too," Mildred said from the doorway as she stepped in and placed some clean clothes on the dresser. "Your Cassie sure is talented, but not as smart as I'd thought."

Nathan's brows dipped as he turned to Mildred. "Oh, she's plenty smart. She just has her own agenda, but what makes you say that?"

"She could be a millionaire. Heck knows your daddy was trying to give her part of the find."

"She deserves it," Nathan offered. "Dad wouldn't have known to drill there if it wasn't for her."

"I agree," Mildred said. "That's why I don't understand it. Cassie wasn't interested in money in her bank account. She said she already has enough."

"If she didn't want money, what did she agree to?"

Mildred shrugged. "That's between her and your daddy. Now wash up. Cassie told me you're taking her to town later."

"Oh, did she now?" Nathan asked, putting away the clean clothes.

"Something about a map and the property appraiser's office."

Nathan's smile grew. "Of course. Why didn't I think of that? They have maps of the entire town. If there's any more heist money, she'll find it."

"That's what she said," Mildred said as she left the room after grabbing a hamper full of towels from the closet. "I'll go heat up your breakfast."

Mildred disappeared while Nathan brushed his teeth and got ready for the day. After jogging down the stairs, he ate and headed out onto the porch where Clayton was sitting.

"About time you woke up," Clayton said. "She's been waiting on you all morning, but judging by her squeals out there, I'd say they struck gold."

"Probably made her a millionaire."

"She's already one. Her entire family is," Clayton said, chuckling as he rose from his seat. "She's like the rest of her sisters. She's got the looks, the heart, and the bank account. And that one isn't naïve either. She's a keeper, Special Agent Murray."

That she was. Nathan's stomach clenched at the memory of almost losing her and the way she'd walked right into what could have been a disastrous situation the previous night. It was like she didn't have a care for her own safety.

Clayton left, claiming he'd be back. He'd promised Amanda a ride into town like she was royalty. He'd lost in a hand of poker.

"Why so glum?" Cassie asked as she jogged over to the porch.

"Looks like you and dad are business partners," Nathan said, gesturing to his father in the field with a couple of guys working the equipment.

"He tried to give me half, but I didn't want it. I wanted something else. He told me I was a fool for not taking it all."

"What was it you wanted?" Nathan asked.

"You'll see." She gave him a wide smile, and her eyes twinkled with mischief. "You ready to go? I thought we could run by the appraiser's office and, later this evening, maybe we can take those people some more food and supplies."

Nathan kissed her temple and took her hand, leading her to the car. "You have a heart of gold."

"Helping people makes me feel good," she said beneath her breath, almost as if she were ashamed of it.

Chapter 20

Nathan's dad tried to convince me that I'd gotten the short end of the stick from the new oil find, but he'd been wrong. When I told him why I wanted what I asked for, I think he finally understood, even if he still thought I deserved more. I didn't.

Nathan parked outside the property appraiser, and within minutes and a couple flashes of his badge, we were settled in a conference room with a plot map of the entire territory, which had streets and addresses for each home.

He stood out of the way while I did my thing using my crystal. I narrowed it down by going over each section, looking for the strongest vibration and arc swing until I was happy. I hunkered over the section and took a deep calming breath, letting the crystal guide me as I asked the questions in my head.

It landed with a thud on the tabletop, Nathan and I leaned over the map looking for the address.

"528 Sycamore Road. You know anyone that lives there?"

Nathan shook his head. "Not yet, but I will."

We left the property office.

"Can we stop and get some food for those people?"

"If we show up at the library, workers might be suspicious why we're there and putting food in their shelter. We might get them in trouble."

I sat back in my seat with a huff. "We have to do something."

He let out a hefty sigh and did a U-turn back in the direction of the fast food places. He ordered for everyone in the basement before we stopped and picked up several boxes of donuts. "What are those for?"

"Aida Mae runs the library. She loves me. I'm going to park around back and take the donuts in while you quickly unload the food. You have to be quick, though, so no one sees you."

Nathan's plan worked like a charm. I startled the people in the shelter for a second when I opened the doors, but that startle quickly turned into relief while Michael and the pastor helped me carry the food. I checked on Mary, and her fever had almost disappeared.

I was waiting in the truck when Nathan returned. "Worked like a charm."

"Looks like it," I said, leaning over to wipe the powdered sugar from his face.

"Everyone still okay down there?"

"Yeah." I sighed. "I just wish they didn't have to live in a dark hole and hide from the world, but I get it."

Nathan started the truck and took my hand, giving it a gentle squeeze. "I promise I'll tell Mildred, and she'll help when we leave. She cooks enough for an army. I'm sure she'll take care of everything, and I'll look into whatever company is coming in here trying to buy up the land. They'll be all right. We'll make sure of it."

Mildred wouldn't need to take care of them, not when my plans were taking shape, not that Nathan needed to know. I wasn't a hundred percent certain that he'd agree with what I had up my sleeve.

We turned down Sycamore Road and passed the address once before circling around and parking a few houses away. Our attempt to look inconspicuous died. A knock on my window made me jump, and my heart raced.

A little old lady with a German shepherd on a leash stood outside the window.

"Crap," Nathan whispered beneath his breath while I rolled the window down.

"Nathan Murray, I thought that was you."

"Mrs. Beatrice, it's good to see you."

"It's been a long time since you used to cut my grass," she said. "Is this your girlfriend that I've heard about?"

"Yes, Mrs. Beatrice, meet Cassie."

"It's a pleasure, dear." She farther into the truck. "I'm head of the neighborhood watch, Nathan, so I check out suspicious people. What are you two doing sitting out here?"

"Nathan is just showing me around town. I told him I might move here, and he's explaining the subdivisions where the good places to live are, in the event I decide to start house hunting."

"Oh, dear, you'd love it here. My neighborhood is kind of quiet. Not much happens around these parts. We've already scared off the troublemakers."

Nathan shook his head. "I hope you went about it legally, Mrs. B."

A sly smile slid onto the woman's face. "It's not illegal to get a suntan, is it? I was wearing a little slip of a bathing suit."

Laughter erupted from my lips, and my hand flew to cover it.

"No, Mrs. B, I guess it's not. I'm sure you'll see Cassie and me again on the street when it turns a little darker. So, just know that we aren't out making trouble."

"Okay, dear. I'm on duty tonight, and I live right there, just in case you've been gone so long that you forgot." She pointed to the house up the block. "I'll make sure that we don't call the law on you."

"That would be appreciated, Mrs. B."

"Anytime, dear." She whistled as she walked off.

I rolled up my window. "She's a character."

"She was one of my eighth-grade teachers." Nathan chuckled. "Whoever lives there is probably working. How about we come back when we have a little bit more cover. Otherwise, everyone on the road is going to come out and talk to us, and we'll lose the element of surprise."

"Wouldn't a simple phone call into the FBI give you the name of who lives there?"

"Sure. But then when I called how I lost the evidence; I was told I was off the case. If I call this in, they'll know I didn't follow orders and I'll probably be in worse trouble."

"Aren't you dying to look around? A portion of that money is around there somewhere. Why didn't you just ask Mrs. Beatrice who lives there? It sounds like that woman would know everyone and everything that happens on these streets."

"I didn't want to tip our hand and give the residents time to pack up and run. We don't know what we're dealing with yet. For all we know, the thieves could have buried it on the property and are coming back to it in a few years when it's not as hot. We don't even know if the homeowners know that it's on the property."

"True. It would be rude to bust through the door and have to witness two old people getting busy."

"Blinding, not rude, Cassie." Nathan chuckled and started the truck.

We knew where it was now, so the waiting was going to be the hardest part. I pulled out my phone and did a search for the address and paid the extra fees for the owner leaving the FBI out of the equation.

"Gentry Holmes mean anything to you?"

"He's the developer that built all of these houses. I doubt he's living in one."

"He's coming up as the owner," I said and turned my phone to show him.

"A couple hours of waiting isn't going to kill us," he teased. "We can run some errands and check on how Amanda's getting things set up in the stall for the competition. She always gets nervous."

"Okay."

Nathan drove down the street. I couldn't help but look back. My stomach was twisting in knots, too, and not from the competition. A sliver of apprehension mixed with worry slid down my spine. Even though I knew I'd be safe with Nathan. I couldn't help but worry that we'd run smack-dab into the person who'd pulled the trigger and killed his mother.

If it were my mother, I wouldn't be able to stop from taking matters into my own hands, and something told me that there was no way that Nathan would listen to reason. There wasn't a reason strong enough not to take revenge.

I'd keep my fingers crossed that we'd find some old folks living there and the money just being stashed somewhere nearby or in the floorboards.

When we arrived at the competition site, everything and everyone was bustling. "They're busy."

"With the competitions tomorrow, it's no wonder. They're running out of time to double and triple check things. I would introduce you around, but they might get annoyed that we're getting in their way."

I chuckled, and we headed to the stall where Nathan and I had given in to our simmering sexual tension. Heat climbed into my cheeks as I stared down into the space. Nathan rested his arms across the stall door and rubbed Obi-Wan's nose.

Nathan leaned in to whisper into my ear. "Are you thinking the same thing I'm thinking?"

I licked my lips as I met his gaze. "I don't think Obi-Wan would like it if we tried to share his stall."

Amanda, Marty, and Pete, one of the roughnecks, were headed in our direction. Amanda stopped in front of us and opened the stall doors. Pete took Obi-Wan by the reins and led him outside.

"What are you two doing here?" Amanda asked.

Marty lifted his thumb over his shoulder. "Amanda, I'm just going to go…I'll see if you're around later."

Amanda's cheeks tinted a pretty pink color that I'm not even sure Nathan recognized. It was so obvious those two had a thing for each other.

"We were checking out an address, but no one was home, so we came to see you," Nathan answered. "How are you holding up?"

"Pete is taking Obi-Wan for a trip around the course to break him in. I was just double-checking I have my saddle and the supplies I need."

"Well, we'll just get out of your way," I said, slipping my palm into the crook of Nathan's elbow.

"I missed the competition in New Orleans, but I could stick around if you want me to give you some tips," Nathan offered.

Amanda's checks tinted more as she glanced in the direction Marty had gone. I followed her gaze and spotted him inside one of the stalls, sticking his head out to see if we were still there.

"Come on, Nathan, you're probably rattling her nerves more than you know. We can see her at dinner."

"Actually, I'm eating out with friends and then we're going dancing, but we can have breakfast together."

Nathan pulled me to a stop. "You shouldn't go out the night before. You need your rest."

"Okay, dad," I teased. "This isn't her first rodeo. She's got this under control."

"Cassie's right. I do," Amanda said, making a shooing motion with her hands.

I led Nathan away, even though he stopped twice and I had to pull to keep him walking. He was finally settled in the truck, and we were now halfway back to his house,

"You like Marty, right?" I asked.

"Sure, he's a good kid. Nothing like how John was growing up. Marty is more of a nerd. He's the type of kid that's going to figure out how to make his horse go faster by studying aerodynamics and statistics and crap."

I grinned. "So, he's a smart one."

"You can say that again."

"That's good."

"Why the sudden interest in Marty?" Nathan asked.

"Because I'm pretty sure he's dating your sister and they're seriously into each other."

Nathan glanced in my direction, and his mouth was parted. "You got all that out of seeing the kid twice?"

"Something like that. Just call it woman's intuition."

"I'm going to kill the kid," he said.

"No, you're not," I teased.

"I'm going to arrest him on suspicion of something," Nathan growled.

"Having a crush on your sister isn't illegal." I chuckled.

Chapter 21

We arrived back at the farm to find Clayton putting his bags in the back of the Town Car. He slammed the trunk as we approached.

"Going somewhere?"

"Duty calls. Ms. Delany has another assignment she needs me on. Are you going to be okay here without me?"

"I don't know how we'll ever manage," I teased and pulled him into a hug. His stance remained awkward and rigid, as though I might give him cooties from the human contact, so I kissed his cheek for good measure and watched in amusement as he wiped the spot with a handkerchief.

"Your sister is still worried about you. She thinks you should leave with me and I should drop you back home."

I gave a nonchalant flip of my wrist. "I'm fine. Go on without me."

Nathan rested his arm over my shoulder and held out a hand to Clayton. "I've got her."

They shook, and Clayton's face softened. "Yeah, I'd say you do."

****

Three hours later, under cover of the cloudy night sky, we parked in the same spot as before, only now lights peeked out from partially closed curtains. Two trucks were parked in the driveway. Nothing unusual there. It was the vehicle of choice in Texas.

Nathan and I sat in silence, watching and waiting, until I couldn't take it anymore. "I'm just going to go peek in the windows. Then we'll know."

I opened the door, and Nathan hurried to turn off the inside overhead light, plunging us back into darkness. "No, you're not."

"It will be fine. You'll be able to see me from the truck." I slipped out of his hold.

"Cassie." He said my name on a loud whisper just as I shut the door.

I jogged across the street and was sliding up next to the shadow of the house when a warm hand landed on my shoulder.

A squeak left my lips before Nathan covered my mouth with his palm and leaned in. "Don't scream. It's just me."

I inched closer to the window on the side of the house, trying to stay out of view of the neighbors. I lifted my head over the windowsill, just enough to peek inside.

"Kitchen," I whispered as I slowly lowered out of view. "Let's try another one."

"This is illegal, Cassie," Nathan whispered as he followed me around toward the back of the house to a sliding glass door.

I peeked around the edge to find John, standing shirtless inside. Kissing him was Murray Ranch roughneck, Pete, who had a towel wrapped around his waist. My hand flew to my mouth to cover my gasp. Poor Monica. Did she know her husband was cheating on her with another man?

"What?" Nathan whispered and moved me out of the way to look inside. He leaned back out of view and pressed his back to the brick. The look on his face and lack of words said it all. Nathan hadn't known either.

He took my hand and hurried me from the house and back across the street. He pulled open the door, and we both froze.

Uncle Dan was sitting in the front seat with a gun pointed at our heads and a phone pressed against his ear. "Get your asses out here."

He motioned with the gun as he slid out of the car. He grabbed my wrist and twirled me to his chest, pressing the gun into my side.

"Why?" Nathan growled and moved closer. Dan cocked the trigger.

"Not out here, kid. I have a reputation to protect," Dan said, just as John and Pete burst out the door and jogged across the street. They were both now fully dressed.

John grabbed Nathan's arm and yanked him toward the house while Dan guided me with the gun.

"You know your son's gay?" I asked, unable to stop myself.

"His little pansy-ass fell in love with the one man more dangerous than himself. I couldn't stop it."

"You cheated on Monica," I called out as they shoved us into the house.

"She doesn't need to know, and she's not going to find out, once I kill you both."

The back of John's fist met my cheek. An explosion of pain stole my breath and sent me to the ground. I was unable to stop the impact. I struggled to breathe as I cupped my hurt face. My fingers came away bloody as I winced.

Nathan reached for me, but froze as John pressed a gun hard against my temple.

"I'm going to kill you, you son of a bitch." Nathan growled.

"You sound like your mother," Dan said as he crossed the room and poured himself a bourbon. "She didn't know how to keep her nose out of my business."

"Which one of you killed her?" Nathan growled as I slowly rose to my feet.

"You might not remember, but your mother and my wife, Tina, were best friends. It was inevitable when our families spent so much time around each other. Your mom was the first to notice the bruises I'd left on Tina. We'd fight, and she'd get me so damn angry." Dan's eyes glazed over as if he were remembering.

"You killed her too, didn't you?" Nathan asked, snapping Dan back into the present. He poured two more drinks and handed one to John and the other to Pete. Without the gun holding me in place, I scooted closer to Nathan's side.

"Your mother killed her when she offered Tina a way out. A way to get away from me. She'd almost made it too, but I caught her just in time. That car accident wasn't difficult to stage."

"Jenna wanted to help Tina hide?" I asked, standing next to Nathan. I rested my palm on his arm, signaling that I was all right.

"That was her thing," Dan said, draining the liquid in the glass. "She has a book of names of others she helped hide. Tina told me about it when I was beating the plan out of her." Dan turned and threw the glass into the fireplace. The shattering sound of glass made me still.

Dan lifted the gun and pointed it at Nathan. "I'd planned the entire bank robbery down to the second. When your mother walked in, that threw everything off. I knew instantly that this was my chance to make her pay."

"You killed her, you son of a bitch." Nathan growled and I held his arm firm.

"I had everything. My plan was already in motion to kill the guys who robbed the bank. The money was all mine. Your mother was just a bonus. I had an air tight alibi. I was a victim just like your mom." He gave Nathan a sadistic grin. "As she lay dying on the floor of the bank, I promised that I'd find her book and contact every one of those men to tell the women's locations."

"You're a sadistic bastard," I said, unable to stop myself.

"Her being at the bank that particular day was kismet. Two birds, wouldn't you say?" Dan let out an evil chuckle as he cocked the trigger again and grinned. "Tell your mom I said hi."

Before he could pull the trigger, Pete shoved the gun to the ground to stop him from shooting. "Don't kill him yet. We could use him."

"I'm not going to help you," Nathan spat.

"How?" John asked.

Pete pistol-whipped Nathan with the butt of the gun. He dropped to his knees, and I went with him, my hands on his face.

"Are you okay?"

"She's how you're going to help us," Pete announced. "Cassie is a freak of nature. She knew where to find oil for William. We're going to use her to find the oil for us, on Michael and Janet's land. You won't have to sell it to the developer to pay off your gambling debts. The oil will be enough to set us up for life," Pete said.

"Then we'll kill Nathan and Monica. The town won't think twice about Cassie leaving town when they find Nathan and Monica dead together in a bed," John said, swiping at his nose. "Pete can kill them both while I establish an unbreakable alibi."

"You won't get away that," I said, helping Nathan to stand. "His family will come looking for us." Not to mention mine when Gwen figured out that I went missing. The entire FDG group would converge on this town. Hopefully, one of my sisters would have a premonition before I died.

Fear skirted my spine. These guys had a plan, and they could probably make it work. I wouldn't let them hurt Nathan, and they knew it. Just like I did. I was falling head over heels for the agent, and that was going to get us both killed.

"Touch him again, and you'll never find a drop," I said, gritting my teeth.

John raised his gun and neared me. He rested his palm on the back of my neck. "You're going to be fun to break."

He leaned over and pressed a hard and punishing kiss to my lips before he pulled away.

I turned my head. "Stronger men than you have tried."

"Oil first, son, then you and Pete can share her like you do with your wife. Let's tie them up in the storm shelter while we devise our plan. After you're finished judging the competition, John, we'll come up with a reason Nathan left town for a few days without saying goodbye. That should give us enough time to set the stage for killing him and Monica in bed. His family will believe me, and then we can get to work. Get Nathan's keys. I need to hide his truck."

They bound our hands behind our backs with zip ties before leading us out back and down into the storm shelter. This storm shelter was being used for storage and was smaller than the one at the library where Michael and Janet were still hiding.

They shoved us down the stairs. I lost my footing, and I landed on my side on the dusty floor seconds before we were plunged into darkness.

Chapter 22

Nathan dropped to his knees beside me. "Are you okay?"

"Yeah," I said, trying to push myself to sit up and ignoring the pain radiating down my arm. "Your friends suck."

Nathan rested his forehead against mine. "They aren't my friends."

He turned his back to me and used his zip-tied hands to help me stand. A scream wretched free as I put pressure on my foot. "I think I sprained my ankle."

Nathan reached for her foot in the darkness and ran his fingers gingerly down to my ankle. "I think you did more than that. Come on let's get you a seat on the stairs so you can take the pressure off your foot."

Nathan started to move around the room, and he'd moved out of my peripheral vision.

"What are you doing?"

"Looking for something sharp to get out of these bindings."

I lifted my butt and slid my wrists beneath, moving my legs through the path until my hands were in front of me. I rose, limping on my foot, and slammed my fists against my legs, tugging each hand in the opposite direction until the plastic snapped free.

Nathan hurried to my side as I wobbled and sat back down. "How did you know to do that?"

"*YouTube* video." I grinned and ran my gaze down his body. "Something tells me you won't be as flexible, so wait here."

I pushed the wall to ease myself up and hopped around the room until I found exactly what I needed. A long thin piece of metal. I returned and slid it through the connection tines, breaking the connection where they could just slide free. Within seconds, he was out.

Nathan kissed me. "You surprise me at every turn."

"I'm kind of unpredictable like that." I sighed. "Okay, I got us free. How are you going to get us out?"

I heard the click sound seconds before light surrounded us. Nathan stood in the middle of the room. He'd pulled the light string hanging from the ceiling. I'd been in worse places than this, but still, knowing what lurked nearby was better than not knowing.

The room had knickknacks of all types lying around. Tools, Christmas decorations, everything you'd think to find stored in a garage back home.

Nathan jogged up the stairs and pushed against the wooden door. It didn't budge.

"Don't suppose you found an ax lying around? Or a key?"

"No," Nathan said, jogging back down the stairs. He opened boxes, looking for a weapon.

Sweat poured down my face as the crystal vibrated against my chest. I slowly rose from my spot and hobbled around the room, almost tripping on a hammer. I picked it up and moved it out of the way. With each step, the vibration would strengthen until I was standing before a locked gun cabinet pressed at the other end of the room.

"Uh, Nathan," I said, clasping my crystal in my hand. "I think I know where your cash is stashed."

I yanked hard on the lock. Breaking locks wasn't a skill that Gwen had taught me yet.

Nathan disappeared before returning to my side with a screwdriver in hand. He pressed the pointy part beneath the hinge bolt holding the door in place, and he pried it up, not stopping until both bolts were removed and the door lay hanging askew by just the lock.

"We work well together," I teased.

He set the door aside and rummaged through the contents. Finding no guns stashed inside was disappointing. Stuff from a kitchen sat on the shelves. Breadboxes, crockpots, steamer pots, everything big and bulky you'd find around a kitchen, including containers for sugar and flour.

He grabbed the cookie jar and opened it, showing that there were stacks of hundreds inside. I tilted the flour canister and lifted the lid and found the same thing. We looked through everything, and in each of those kitchen storage items, they had stacks of clean hundred-dollar bills with no red dye, until we got to the breadbox.

Nathan pulled it out and had a hard time opening it. He tilted it and pulled out stained cash. "Looks like more than one teller got their dye packs inside."

I picked up another pot, and when I did, it sounded full of loose change. I peeked beneath the lid, and my heart clenched. I showed Nathan. Sitting inside were a few of the gold coins that my client had found. These men really had killed Herbert.

Nathan pulled out a fistful of the ruined money in his grasp. "I'm sure Dan had an idea of which bags full of cash would get ruined."

Nathan sat back on his haunches and exhaled a long deep breath. The mystery of his mother's death was solved, but he'd yet to bring the criminals to justice. All of the original bank robbers were dead. Dan had seen to that. Only the fourth man was still breathing, but not for long.

"Did you know anything about a book?"

"Yeah, my dad told me about it three years ago. My mom was part of an underground system that helped battered women disappear and start new lives. She had a ledger of everyone they helped. We thought she died over that. She'd gone to the bank to retrieve it and brought it home to add another woman to the list. I don't think my dad realized who it was. My mom returned back to the bank the next day with other items in her backpack to put in the safety deposit box. The book stayed at the house. She needed time to get the details figured out and written in. If my mom hadn't returned to the bank to put more stuff into her deposit box, she might still be alive."

"Something tells me that Dan wouldn't have left that to chance."

"You're right." Nathan's jaw ticked as he answered.

"And I guess Tina never made it out of town or got her name in the ledger."

"My mom died for trying to help her, though. Funny thing is that she didn't even tell my dad who she was trying to help. We hadn't a clue." Fury filled Nathan's voice. "We went on fucking family vacations with those people. We'd camped together, done everything together."

"Let's hope Marty isn't anything like them."

"Amanda," Nathan whispered as if remembering that there was still a family connection.

"They won't hurt her. They have to keep up appearances," I said, resting my hand on his. "My sisters will come looking for us. I'm sure of that."

"We need to get out of here." Nathan rose with renewed purpose and continued his search around the area.

I stumbled, and Nathan was quick to my side. "You rest, and I'll do the heavy lifting."

I sat back down, ignoring the throb in my foot and the sweat beading on my brow. I couldn't imagine having to live down here in a confined space. Michael and Janet were much stronger than I could ever be.

Chapter 23

I'd fallen asleep sometime watching him pace the room. When I'd woken up, I was leaning against his shoulder. He'd made a blanket out of winter coats and had covered my body.

I glanced up at him to find a look of defeat on his face.

"No luck finding us a way out?" I asked.

"I came up with a plan, but it could kill us," he said deadpanned, as if he'd been debating on telling me.

"What do you have in mind?"

"We need someone to find us." He glanced in the direction of the gas cans across the room. "We could start a fire with the money and wait until the cavalry arrives.

My mouth parted. "The smoke inhalation would kill us first, but you might be on to something. What if we set fire to one of the doors instead of the objects in this room?"

"It wouldn't matter," Nathan said, running his fingers over his head. "We'd still end up dead if the fire department didn't get here in time."

"Okay." I sighed. "What if we pretended to still be tied up when they come back? What if we rushed them with a weapon?" I spotted the hammer across the room that I'd moved out of the way. The handle was partially sticking out from beneath a small dresser.

"What weapon?" he asked, rising and almost knocking me over. "I've looked through every box in here. I've torn this place apart."

I made an O with my lips. "I almost tripped on it when I was following the crystal. I shoved it beneath that small table. Sorry."

Nathan kissed my lips. A look of relief filled his eyes. "You're beautiful and smart, and I love you, Cassie Bennett. If we get out of this, you're going to be spending a lot more time with me."

"Promises, promises." I chuckled and watched Nathan pick up the hammer and head back up the stairs.

He slammed it against the door, over and over again. Each stroke sent shards of wood flying. The loud sound was deafening.

"Aren't you afraid they'll hear you?" I asked.

Nathan swung harder. "Nope, I don't think anyone's home. John will be at the rodeo competition. Dan will be at the bank, and even if Pete is home, I can take him, but I suspect he's with my dad or Amanda." Nathan swung harder and faster until he broke through. A gush of air rushed in, and the sun shined down. Nathan used the claw part of the hammer to tear a piece big enough for him to climb through.

"Wait here," he said and grabbed the screwdriver, disappearing outside. Within seconds, the door was pulled off the hinges and freedom was in sight.

"Wait there, and I'll carry you out," he said.

I wobbled over to the money and shoved it into an empty gym bag lying nearby. I wrapped it around my neck when Nathan returned. His gaze fell on the empty kitchen stuff before returning to meet mine with a smile.

"They're going to be so pissed."

"I know." I chuckled as Nathan swept me up into his arms and carried me out of the storm shelter and straight to Mrs. B's house.

He knocked on the door, and she opened it. Her eyes widened. "What have you two been doing?"

"Mrs. B, I need to use your phone, please."

"Come in. Come in." The woman moved out of the way, and Nathan eased me down into a kitchen chair before disappearing to use the phone.

"Can I get you something?"

"Water and a gun would be great." I coughed as I spoke. "Your neighborhood isn't so safe, after all."

She hurried to get water and returned with it a second later, along with a shotgun, and placed them both on the table.

I loved this woman. She was old enough to be my Grams and was filled with gumption too.

She and my Grams would probably get along great if they didn't kill each other first.

I ignored the water and checked the chamber on the gun first. My eyes closed as I downed the entire bottle of water, barely stopping for air.

The look on Mrs. Beatrice's face was priceless.

"You want more, dear?"

I swiped my mouth with the back of my hand to catch any droplets. Nathan appeared at the table. He picked up the gun and moved to stand by the window, peeking out. "Police and paramedics will be here in five minutes. FBI in an hour."

"I don't need a paramedic. I'm fine," I said, hobbling to stand. "We have people to arrest."

Nathan glanced over at me and raised a brow. "Paramedics and police first. Then we'll deal with everything else."

"Okay, but promise me that I'll get to see John in handcuffs."

Mrs. Beatrice's mouth parted. "John and Monica, John? They're friends with Pete, who lives just across the street."

"They're more than just friends." I winked at the woman as I hopped on one foot over to sit on the couch and rested my foot on the cushion. I'd stayed there until the police and paramedics arrived.

"Oh my. People are going to think I've kicked the bucket with all the action on the street."

"It's okay, Mrs. Beatrice. You can brag about helping an FBI agent solve a decade-old case and catching bank thieves."

Chapter 24

Because I'd been taken to the hospital, I missed the final takedown. But I heard about it afterward. John had been arrested in the middle of the rodeo competition and taken into custody by the FBI. When they'd searched his house, they found Monica unconscious in her bed and barely alive with an empty liquor bottle in her hands and a half empty vial of pills by her side. It's almost like she knew the end was near.

They'd chased Pete down to Nathan's daddy's farm. He'd been working as if nothing was amiss in the world. Dan had been hauled out of the bank in handcuffs.

Federal charges of robbery, kidnapping, murder, and attempted murder awaited all of them. Each would be going away for a long time.

I'd spent my time wasting away in the hospital waiting for a doctor to wrap my ankle. It had been a sprain just like I thought, but it took an x-ray before Nathan and the doctors were convinced.

I'd been relieved of the bag containing the robbery money. Only six hundred thousand out of a million had been recovered. Maybe one day when the wind died down, I might go snooping for the remainder if they hadn't spent it.

Back at Nathan's house, I resigned myself to the porch, staring out at the equipment in the field. My leg was propped up on the swing, taking up the length of the cushion as I faced the open field.

The entire family missed the benefit because of everything that happened. Mildred went in their place. I was sure the town would understand when word got out. It was like the Murrays had to mourn Jenna all over again.

Nathan moved my leg and sat down next to me, putting my foot in his lap. He kissed me. "The FBI needs me to report in."

"I figured." I smiled up at him and laid my head on the back of the swing. "I'm not leaving just yet. Your dad said I could stay as long as I wanted."

Nathan caressed my hair. "You know I was serious about you and me being an actual thing."

"Describe *thing*," I teased just as the porch door opened.

William Murray came strolling out with Amanda. She sat on the railing and hugged one of the beams. She was wearing the shiny new belt buckle she'd won from competition.

William took a seat next to dad, who I don't think had moved from his seat the entire time I'd been in town.

William leaned in and handed Nathan a leather-bound book. "That was your mom's. It's got the names of everyone she helped disappear. Keep it safe, son. If Dan knew about the book, there's no telling if he told anyone else. It's no longer safe on the property."

"What's going to happen to Marty?" Amanda asked.

"He's eighteen years old and a good kid. He'll probably go stay with his aunt," Nathan said.

Amanda frowned. Sadness filled her eyes.

"You know, long distance relationships can work. I'm sure you'll even see him at other competitions and rodeos," I said trying to offer more hope.

"I guess," she said as she met my gaze.

"Don't worry, Amanda Panda. I'll make sure he's taken care of and not lost in the shuffle, and I'll tell you where he lands. He didn't have anything to do with our mom's death. He shouldn't be penalized for who his father is," Nathan said.

A little bit of hope shined through her hazel eyes.

Nathan and I stayed on the swing most of the day, doing nothing more than talking and being with each other. We'd bonded, and I'd fallen for him. We'd gone from almost dying together, to saving each other, to solving a murder. We were a fantastic team. How in the heck we'd make any type of relationship work, going forward, I hadn't a clue. But now I understood Amanda's stance.

Nathan had packed and pulled the suitcase onto the porch. His dad had the keys in his hand and patted his son on the back before he grabbed the luggage. Nathan closed the distance between us. He leaned down and kissed me. "I don't know when I'll be back."

I cupped his cheeks and kissed him. "That's probably good. I don't know where I'll be, you know…in case you're interested in finding me."

"Cassie, I love you." His words were a whisper before he walked off.

He left me speechless on the porch, staring after them and the dust being kicked up as they drove away.

"That boy knows how to go in for the kill, just like my daughter, his momma," the old man announced.

My head reared back at the sound of his raspy, little used voice. "And here I thought this whole time that you were William's daddy."

"Nope," he said matter-of-factly. "Jenna's first husband was a sorry piece of dog crap, and she told me she was going to run because he hit her. She hid it for a long time until one of her friends realized what was going on. This was a long time ago, but that's what started us down this crazy path. She just had to find the will to leave, and no way was I letting my baby girl go running off without me. Although I offered to kill for her, she wouldn't let me do it."

"She didn't want you to go to jail." My heart clenched at the thought. Had someone been beating on one of my sisters. I'd offer the same thing.

"That book got passed down from one person to the next. Each new organizer pledges to keep the names safe. That's where his momma used to disappear to every year on her birthday. They'd all meet up and she'd check in on the others trying to decide on her replacement."

"I'm sure Nathan will take care of it."

The old man tsked and rose from his spot. He crossed the distance between us and pulled out a piece of paper from his pocket. "That book Nathan has is written in code. In order to decipher it, and carry on the Murray tradition of being a savior, you're going to need the key."

"Oh, I couldn't," I said, even as I reached for the paper.

"You already saved him, and you're about to save the people under the library. You'll save some battered women too. I have faith in you."

"Wait, how did you know about the library?"

"William told me what you bargained for from the oil location. You wanted the land to build some tiny homes for those people that lost everything. It might be a great place for someone who might, one day, need to disappear, even if it's a pit stop, don't you think? Michael and Janet will be great hosts."

My mouth parted. It took a lot to make me speechless, but the old man had definitely done that.

He did know my secrets; he did know everything I had planned. Well, almost everything. I smiled.

Within a week of Nathan being gone, the tiny houses I'd bought were delivered to the acreage William had transferred to me. The permits had been secured, and the entire town had helped to get everything up and running. The sign above the entrance read, Jenna's Place. A sign in the field read *In loving memory of a woman who gave up everything to help others.*

In my heart, I aspired to be like her one day. I didn't stick around the farm after that. I wasn't one for tearful goodbyes. Amanda drove me to the airport and helped me pass the time for boarding.

"He should be back any day. Are you sure you don't want to wait around?"

I nudged her shoulder. "He knows how to reach me. Besides I'm sure your family could use some peace and quiet. Once the reporters get wind that I've left, they'll leave you alone."

"You are kind of a celebrity around here now. You should stay and live it up."

"I'll take a hard pass," I whispered just as the announcements came over that my flight was ready to board. I rose and grabbed my bag and pulled her into a hug. "You keep looking out for them, okay?"

"You know I will. It's a full-time job."

I pulled a house key out of my pocket and dangled it in front of her.

"What's this?"

"I signed a new tenant for Jenna's Place. I thought maybe you could welcome him."

"Who?"

"Marty." I grinned. "His flight is due in twenty minutes. Across the field should be close enough to keep seeing each other, don't you think?"

Amanda threw her arms around my neck and hugged me as she danced a bouncy jig. She stopped and stared into my eyes. "You're serious."

"I wouldn't kid about that," I answered as she bounced up and down again before releasing me.

Her hand went to her hair. "Oh, God. I'm not wearing any makeup. I'd barely brushed my hair."

"He's not going to care, I promise," I said as I hobbled over to the gate and handed over my ticket. I gave one more glance over my shoulder to watch Amanda smiling as she waved. I'd see her again one day. The next time the well ran dry and they needed help in finding the pay dirt.

KATE ALLENTON

Chapter 25

I walked out of the courtroom with a huge smile. Bill Tanner's face would be seen on TV tonight, but it wouldn't be on the ten o'clock news. Nope, he got more than a slap on the wrist for hitting me and pulling a gun. Especially when the FBI showed the surveillance videos. Mrs. Tanner's divorce would be finalized tomorrow. Today was a good day. Had this been how Jenna felt when helping those women?

I pushed out of the courthouse, got into my car, and drove home.

Getting out, I smiled at Nathan sitting on my porch.

"How was court?" he asked as he rose from his spot and met me halfway.

"Justice was served," I answered.

"Well, we were a major force in the apprehension of the weatherman."

My mouth parted, and I tapped his stomach. "You weren't even watching him. You were watching me watch him."

Nathan chuckled and pulled me into his arms. "Watching you was the best job I ever had."

I rolled my eyes, and he pulled me in and kissed me slow and melt-worthy until I leaned into his hold.

"Jenna's Place?" he asked.

"You mom deserves to be remembered, even if she couldn't publicly announce she was behind helping over a hundred women disappear."

"Marty?" he asked next.

"Amanda loves him, and I figured you wouldn't want her traipsing across the world following him. It's better he's nearby for everyone involved."

"And Michael and Janet and the others. Those are some pretty cool little digs until they get back on their feet. You have a big heart, Cassie Bennett."

I reached behind his neck and guided him to my mouth. "My sister had a premonition about us after I got back."

"Are you sure it was a real premonition and not a little birdy that whispered in her ear?" He arched a brow.

"Well now, I don't know." I moved to sit on the porch swing that now served as a reminder to slow down and enjoy the view.

He didn't sit beside me. Instead, he kneeled in front of me and opened the blue Tiffany box in his hand. "Did it have to do with a ring?"

My lips widened into a smile. "Maybe, but you know we could be all wrong for each other."

"Or maybe perfect for each other. You're my dimes. My hopes, my wishes. We can have a long engagement, and you can spend time getting to know me, but I already know I love you, Cassie Bennett."

"You have this all figured out, don't you?"

"You found my heart, Cassie. I'm hoping that you'll keep it."

I held out my trembling hand and smiled. "I plan to do just that."

He started to slide it on my finger and paused. "Is that a yes?"

I nodded. "Absolutely, yes."

Never in a million years had I believed I'd find true love just by working my job, and even now, with Nathan by my side, my sister's premonition had been clear; we'd be helping a ton more men and women on our quest. I patted my pocket where an extra crystal was stashed, along with the decryption code. This was a new chapter in our life. One that promised things I would have never even imagined.

Two hours later, I left Nathan asleep in my bed and fixed a cup of coffee, staring at the map on the table and the ceramic stone sitting on top, engraved with the name Bennett.

I'd been trying for days to find our relatives without a hint of luck. Nothing to show where this other line might be.

Next to it was one of Talia's friendship bracelets, which she'd always worn. Butterflies and fear had me waiting to try anything with that one. If Gwen was right, Talia was still alive somewhere in the world. She would have grown up believing… what exactly?

"Is that the Bennett genealogy project you were telling me about?" Nathan asked as he moved behind me and wrapped his arms around my waist.

"Yeah, and like the others, I'm not having any luck."

Nathan kissed my temple. "Maybe you're going about it all wrong. Maybe there's an easier way."

"Easier than me working with my crystal?" I asked.

"It's called DNA, honey." Nathan took the coffee from my hands and set it on the table. He turned me in his arms and kissed my lips before answering. "Submit your DNA sample to the genealogy site. Our forensic and investigation departments are using them more and more every day. All it takes is for one of your relatives searching for their roots, and you may get a hit."

I nestled into Nathan's hold and whispered against his chest. "I love you, Nathan."

"I love you too, Cassie, and I can't wait to make you my wife," he answered, kissing the top of my head.

READ MORE BY KATE ALLENTON

ALL BOOKS ARE IN KINDLE UNLIMITED

EACH FINISHED SERIES IS IN A BOX SET FOR EASY READING.

Not sure which series you want to start with? Get my Mystic Secrets Starter Box Set for **ONLY 99 pennies**! Three books that are all the first in their series!

Love your romance with a supernatural twist? Check out Skylar

Or maybe you like your Romantic Suspense without the supernatural additive. Then Check out Deception.

GO READ THEM ALL FOR FREE WITH YOUR KINDLE UNLIMITED SUBSCRIPTION!

About the Author

Kate has lived in Florida for most of her entire life. She enjoys a quiet life with her husband, Michael and two kids.

Kate has pulled all-nighters finishing her favorite books and also writing them. She says she'll sleep when she's dead or when her muse stops singing off key.

She loves creating worlds full of suspense, secrets, hunky men, kick ass heroines, steamy sex and the love of a lifetime. Not to mention an occasional ghost and other supernatural talents thrown into the mix.

Sign up for her newsletters at www.kateallenton.com

She loves to hear from her readers by email at KateAllenton@hotmail.com, on Twitter @KateAllenton, and on Facebook at facebook.com/kateallenton.1

Made in the USA
Columbia, SC
16 August 2022

65423925R00136